Rough Stock

Book 2 Cowboy Code Series

Lauren Fraser

Blurb

Professional cowboy Brody Kyle was at the top of his game before an injury changed everything.
Now if he wants the chance to win, he needs the help of horse trainer Denise Shaw. But when he's around this strong, sexy woman the gold buckle is the last thing on his mind.

Denise has spent her life proving she's as good as any man. Nothing fazes her. So what is
it about Brody that instantly turns her into a giggling girl and sets her blood on fire? She needs some time between the sheets to get him out of her system. Unfortunately, the heat between them only makes her crave him more.

Brody has never become emotionally involved with a woman, but something about Denise gets past
his defenses. There's nothing sexier than seeing an

in-control woman submit in the bedroom and be so kickass everywhere else.

Their casual fling soon becomes much more and they must find a way to balance control if they're to have a shot at forever.

Contents

Chapter One

The Thunderhead Ranch sign loomed in front of him as Brody Kyle turned his truck off the highway onto the winding road that would lead him to his destination. He tapped his fingers on the steering wheel along to the beat of the death metal song pounding through the stereo. Since he was a cowboy, everyone assumed he'd be into country music and line dancing, and he was when it impressed the ladies, but given the choice he'd take the hard, driving beat of metal any day.

Even with the stereo cranked, he still couldn't drown out his thoughts. What if she said no? His nerves twisted in his gut. This had to work.

After his horse had fallen during the final trials of the season and shattered his leg, Brody knew his only chance at success on the tour this year would be to convince Denise Shaw to work with him and his new horse. Without her, his horse would never be ready in time. And he needed to compete in as many events as he could to stand the best chance. There was no way he would get the buckle if he only managed to hit the end of the season.

He'd been dreaming big for so long he could practically taste the victory, the weight of the gold buckle in his hand and how being the champion would feel. Not only to show everyone who said he'd never amount to anything that they were wrong, but to be able to afford to have something real that was his and could never be taken from him. He'd do whatever it took to make that a reality.

Brody could almost picture the ranch he planned to buy. But without competing on the tour, he'd never have enough money in the bank to comfortably own his own spread free and clear. Sure he could afford something now, but getting it up and running and maintaining it was a whole other issue.

No, he needed at least another season or two of winning to have enough in the bank to carry him through. And without Denise that wasn't going to happen.

The only problem was Denise wasn't like other women. She seemed hell bent on ignoring the attraction between them. Which wasn't going to work in his favor.

He'd been trying to wrangle a date with her for two years, ever since he'd first laid eyes on her. But she wanted no part of it. Hopefully, she wouldn't let that stand in the way of her helping him.

After several minutes, the Shaw homestead came into view. The rambling ranch house with the wide porch was the kind of home Brody had always dreamed of as a kid. Instead, he'd grown up in a ramshackle trailer, which shook every time the wind blew. Unfortunately, the trailer he'd grown up in had been in better shape than his family's ranch, which was probably why the bank had repossessed the property. Losing their home had been the beginning of the end for his family.

In the circular drive, Brody pulled his truck to a stop and jumped down from the cab. He scanned the area around the house, wondering which way he should go in order to find Denise. The barn was probably his best bet.

Before he'd taken more than a half-dozen steps, a lean figure exited the barn. Brody grinned when he saw Duncan.

"Hey," he called out.

A smile spread across Duncan's face. Brody walked toward the other man and the two met somewhere in the middle.

"Hey, man, what are you doing here?" Duncan asked.

"I'm here to see Denise."

In an instant, the friendly smile left his face. "Why do you want to see her?"

What the hell? Was there something going on between Denise and Duncan that he wasn't aware of? He hoped not.

"I want to talk to her about training my new horse."

Duncan's posture relaxed instantly. "Yeah, sorry, man. I heard about Buster taking that fall. You okay?"

Brody's chest gripped tight, squeezing his heart. He'd lost not only his chance at winning but he'd lost a part of himself that day. So, no, he wasn't okay.

Putting Buster down had been like killing his best friend. But how did you admit that to someone, even another cowboy, without sounding like a total wuss? It was his horse, not a family member, despite how much it felt like it. He clenched his jaw tightly. Damn, he hated feeling like this.

Instead of admitting it, he shrugged. "Knee took a bit of a beating, but overall I'm fine." He glanced toward the corral where he assumed Denise worked with the horses. "If Denise can turn my new horse into half the roper Buster was I'll be good and make a run for it again this year."

Duncan clasped a hand on Brody's shoulder and gave it a quick squeeze in a show of support.

Crap, so much for not looking like a wuss.

"If anybody can get your horse ready it's Dee." Duncan glanced over Brody's shoulder toward the truck. "You got him in the back?"

"Yeah, figured Denise wouldn't know if she was willing unless she had a look first."

Duncan snorted. "There isn't a horse around that Dee can't work with. No one's got her touch." A smile spread across Duncan's face as if he was remembering how her touch felt. Brody's knuckles flexed into a fist at the idea of the other man touching the woman he'd wanted for so long.

This was going to be fucking unbearable if Denise and Duncan were an item. He exhaled hard. Somehow he'd have to handle it. Without Denise's help, he didn't stand a chance of winning all-around cowboy next year.

He needed those cash prizes. And without the winnings, there'd be no huge endorsements, which meant he'd be dragging tail for several more years to earn the money he needed to buy his own place outright. He'd been so close this year until Buster got hurt and everything fell to shit.

Brody looked around the yard again. Where was she? "Is Denise around?"

Duncan laughed. "Yeah, she went in to grab a shower."

"In the middle of the day?"

Duncan snorted. "It was umm...kind of a necessity. Come on, I'll take you inside."

Denise pushed the glass shower door open and pulled a plush, pale-blue towel off the warmer. She wrapped it around her body then pulled the smaller towel off the rack and twisted it around her hair.

"You need me to wash your back, darlin'?" Duncan's rumbling voice bellowed down the hallway.

Her head snapped up at the sound of his amused voice. She snarled, remembering the way he'd laughed himself silly while she lay covered in manure after slipping on the ground. Next time she'd step on the damn dog's tail and be done with it. "If you come anywhere near me, Duncan Kane, you won't be able to sit on your horse for a month, let alone do anything else."

The jerk hadn't even given her a hand up. Finally, he'd held out the end of his shovel for her to grab on to so he could pull her up since he didn't want to touch her. Not that she could blame him, but that was beside the point.

"Come on, it can't be any worse than some of those potions you're always putting on your face. Don't some of those have bat dung in 'em? What's the difference?" Duncan asked.

Oh, he was going to pay. She stormed out of the bathroom, wielding her hair brush to whack him. As she rounded the corner, she stopped dead in her tracks. Holy shit, Brody Kyle. Her hand immediately went to her hair and she ripped the towel turban off her head.

She closed her eyes and groaned. Oh god, could this get more embarrassing? A normal person would have covered themselves up immediately, but no, not her, she instantly thought of how stupid she must look with a fuzzy, pink-cheetah-print towel on her head. This was mortifying.

"Hi, Denise." Brody's whiskey-roughened voice glided over her skin like a caress. What was it about him that immediately turned her into a bumbling *girl*? She was a strong woman who could hold her own with any man on the ranch but within seconds of being around Brody Kyle she was a giggly twit who couldn't control herself. Probably why she usually avoided him like the plague. Well that and his "love 'em and leave 'em" reputation.

She pressed the towel against her chest. The last thing she needed was for it to fall. That would just be the icing on the humiliation cake.

"You sure I can't dry your back, Dee?" Duncan teased. She opened her eyes and looked at him. He grinned and waggled his eyebrows ridiculously at her. How could she stay mad at him?

She laughed. "No, you big loser, you can't dry my back. If you want to be helpful, go clean up the shit."

Duncan shrugged. "Ah well, can't blame a guy for trying." He turned halfway around then touched his finger to his cheek. "Ah, Dee, you missed a spot."

Oh my god, no. Her hands flew to her face and the offending mark. The second she let go of her towel it fell to the floor. With a squeal, she grabbed it, clasped it in front of her and tore off down the hall, knowing full well her ass was completely on display. Better her ass than her front.

She slammed the bedroom door and flopped onto her bed, completely mortified. Brody Kyle had seen her run buck-ass naked out of a room. *Just shoot me now.* Not only that, but Duncan had witnessed the whole thing. She'd never live this down. *Oh god, please don't let my ass have been jiggly.*

Denise sat up and looked at herself in the mirror. Her face was a flaming red but other than that it was clean. Son of a bitch. "I'm going to kill you, Duncan," she yelled.

His chuckling reply drifted through the closed door. "It was worth it, darlin'. I'm heading back out. Brody will be in the kitchen waiting for you, so don't take too long."

She flopped onto her bed again. No, no, no, she did not want to have to face Brody again today. This day sucked!

Duncan turned to Brody and pinned him with a look. "You didn't see anything," Duncan ordered.

"Yeah right." He snorted. The sight of Denise's firm, ripe ass bolting down the hallway was not something he would ever forget. The slow sizzle of awareness burned from his brain down to his cock. The only thing that would have been better was if she'd walked instead of run so he would've had more time to admire the view.

Brody glanced down the hallway and a slow smile spread across his face. No, he definitely wasn't going to forget.

Duncan growled beside him. "I mean it, Brod, forget about it."

At the hostile tone of Duncan's voice, Brody turned toward the other man. "Why? What's it to you?"

"We're friends."

"Friends? Is that all?"

"Of course, that's all. Dee is Justin's sister. She's not...god no...we're friends, that's it."

"If you two are just friends then why do you care how I'm looking at her?"

"Because Dee deserves a hell of a lot better than you."

Brody squared his shoulders as he looked at the other man. A man he'd thought was his friend. "What the hell is that supposed to mean?"

"Come on, Brody, we both know what you're like with women." Duncan shook his head. "Dee's not like that, she's different."

"Christ, Dunc, I wasn't going to ask her to service the whole tour." He wasn't a complete Neanderthal. He did know the difference between a nice girl and one who wasn't. And Denise was definitely a good girl. One he'd like to corrupt a little but who could blame him?

Duncan glared at him. "You better not be asking her to service *you*."

Jesus, Duncan had a low opinion of him. Well who the hell was he to judge? It's not as if he hadn't been with his share of women. Shit, they'd had threesomes together a couple of times over the years. And Dunc hadn't complained when Brody had put his roping skills to use at the request of one of the bunnies. Then it was all great. He'd even taught Duncan how to tie the ropes for future reference.

But now suddenly his sexual preferences weren't cool. Screw that.

Pissed, Brody stepped in closer to Duncan, challenging him. "Why not? What are you going to do about it if I am?"

Duncan moved forward and drilled his finger into Brody's chest. He poked him so hard Brody was surprised Duncan's finger didn't pop out through his back.

"Dee's family. You hurt her, and friend or not, I'll kick your ass," Duncan growled and pressed his finger deeper into Brody's chest. "When I'm done beating the shit out of you, Kase and Jus will each want a turn too."

"Duncan." Denise's angry voice broke through the tension in the room. "What do you think you're doing?"

Duncan glanced over Brody's shoulder and grimaced. "Hey, Dee, I didn't see you there."

"Clearly," she snapped. She looked between the two men, her eyes narrowed to tiny slits.

Brody bit back a smirk when Duncan lowered his head and looked at the ground rather than at Denise. She looked formidable.

Denise stormed over to Duncan and shoved him in the chest. "What the hell, Dunc?"

Duncan shrugged.

"No, don't shrug. I get you and my brother feel like it's your job to protect me. It was annoying in high school but it's damn right insulting now. I'm a big girl and I can make my own decisions. If I want to grab Brody and fuck him against the wall I will."

Brody's dick twitched beneath his jeans. He definitely liked the sound of that. When she looked over at him, he flashed her a grin.

Denise rolled her eyes. "Don't get any ideas, cowboy."

She turned back to Duncan. "And if I want him to take a hike, I'll tell him. I don't need you or anyone else telling me what I can and can't do. You're my friend, not my keeper, Dunc."

Duncan nodded slowly. "You're right. I'm sorry, Dee." He raised his head until he was looking at her. She rolled her eyes again. Dunc smiled then glanced over at Brody and scowled. "I just didn't like the way he was looking at you."

Denise laughed. "How was he looking at me?"

Duncan's lip curled up in a snarl. "Like he'd been in the desert for days and finally found water."

Denise's eyes widened and her head snapped back. She slowly looked over at Brody and whatever she saw reflected on his face made her blush.

Damn, he wasn't that bad. Sure he wanted her but he wasn't panting after her like a dog in heat. Feigning nonchalance, he ran his gaze down her body. "What can I say, Denise? You've got a great ass."

She narrowed her eyes.

What? I'm only human.

She shook her head and turned to Duncan. "If you don't like him looking, maybe you shouldn't have tricked me into dropping the towel. Hell, you probably looked too so you can't really be pissed if Brody did the same."

Duncan grinned. "Of course I looked. Just 'cuz you're Jus' sister doesn't mean I'm dead. You looked good, Dee."

"Ugh, you are so frustrating," she groaned. Planting her hands on her hips, she glared at him. "Like I said, I'm a grown woman now. I can take care of myself. So let me make my own decisions."

"Fine," he grumbled. "But if he hurts you—"

"If something happens with Brody, it's my decision and I'll deal with any consequences that might arise. Got it?"

"Yes ma'am," Duncan murmured.

"Good. Now get out of here and go back to work," she ordered.

Duncan wrapped his arms around Denise and hugged her. He whispered something in her ear Brody couldn't quite hear. She sighed loudly then hugged Duncan back.

Feeling like an interloper as he watched the byplay between the two, Brody scanned the living room. His gaze landed on the slew of pictures on the mantel. Family. Roots. The green-eyed monster stabbed him in the chest. He'd never had anything even close to that. He sure as heck didn't have a stack of family photos to hang up. He didn't even have one. Someday he'd have that for himself. That's why he needed Denise's help. To win.

The pair pulled apart and Duncan turned to look at Brody. He pointed his finger and said, "Remember what I said."

"Yep, got it," Brody replied.

The door snicked shut behind Duncan, leaving them alone together. Pushing the sexual attraction to the background, Brody rocked back on his heels and focused on the task at hand. What was he going to do if she said no? He took a deep breath and exhaled. It just wasn't an option.

Denise placed her hands on her hips and stared him down. "All right, Brody, spill it. Why are you here?"

Chapter Two

"I need your help."

His deep, rugged voice slid across her skin. Damn, what was it about him that turned her into this walking hormone the second he got within sight? She was a strong, confident woman, but somehow Brody dissolved her into mush. Not that she'd ever let him know. Hell no, the last thing she needed was him holding it over her.

She'd grown up surrounded by macho men, but somehow Brody made them all seem like pushovers. There was something that lingered in the depths of his eyes, a wildness, something untamed that called to her and scared the shit out of her at the same time. And because of it she always tried to keep her distance.

"My help? Why would you need my help?"

"Because you're the best and that's what I need."

"Why? I thought you'd always trained your horses yourself."

"I have."

He stuck his hands in the front of his worn jeans, drawing her attention to his muscular thighs. She bit back a sigh. *Focus, Dee, focus.* "So why do you need me?"

"I don't know... After what happened with Buster." He shook his head slowly.

Denise frowned. "What happened with Buster wasn't your fault. He got caught up in the dirt. It could have happened to anyone."

"Maybe."

She could feel the raw emotion churning inside him from her place across the room. She stepped closer and before she thought better of it she placed her hand on his arm. "It was an accident, Brod," she said softly.

He looked down at her hand. She pulled it away and put her hand behind her back to stop herself from touching him again.

When he looked back at her, his eyes were tortured. Whatever was going on with him was enough to humble him into asking for help. The Brody Kyle she knew didn't ask anyone for anything. He seemed to be able to do everything by himself and usually better than anyone else. Kind of like her dad, which she'd learned the hard way wasn't a good thing.

"I need help if I'm going to be ready in time and you're my best hope."

She grimaced. "I'm sorry, Brody, I think you wasted a trip. From what I heard, Buster's not ever going to be able to compete."

"Yeah, no, he's not. I had to put him down."

Oh god, that must have been horrible. Growing up on a ranch meant putting animals down was part of life, but it wasn't something she'd ever been able to get used to.

To her animals were like family and her dad hadn't been able to beat that notion out of her no matter how hard he'd tried. Every time they'd had to put an animal down she'd bawled despite her father yelling at her to shut up and quit being a baby. She couldn't remember how many times she'd heard how useless she was as a rancher and how he wished she'd been another son.

The pain that briefly flashed on Brody's face made her wonder if he wasn't a little more like her than she'd originally thought. "I'm really sorry. That must have been really hard."

"Yeah, well." He sighed. "That's why I need you. I bought a new horse and I need him tuned up and ready to compete by March if I'm going to make a run for my buckle this year."

"March? That's only two months away."

"I know. He's trained he's just not... He's not Buster, you know?"

Denise rubbed her face. Two months wasn't very long but if she could get the horse ready and help Brody land a gold buckle, people would be coming from all over to get her to train for them. She'd be crazy to pass up the chance. But two months?

"What am I starting with?" she asked.

"Why don't we head outside and I'll show you."

"You brought the horse with you?"

He flicked his hand in that "yeah well," kind of way. "Figured you couldn't make a decision without knowing what you were getting."

"Fine," she said. "Let's go." She gestured to the door. Once on the porch, she shoved her feet into her filthy boots. As she made her way down the stairs, she glanced at the huge trailer that filled the driveway. "Moving in?" she asked.

Brody grinned. "You asking?"

She rolled her eyes. "Just show me the horse."

He walked around to the back of the trailer, opened the door and dropped the ramp. The trio of horses inside nickered.

The buckskin in the first stall kicked against the wall of the trailer.

"Easy, boy," Brody said and reached out his hand to the horse.

Going on instinct, Denise followed Brody into the trailer. "This is your new guy?" she asked, watching the way the horse eyed Brody warily.

"It's that obvious?"

"Yep." She stepped in closer. "What's his name?"

"Rex."

The horse snorted at the mention of his name. "He's beautiful. How old?"

"Seven."

"He's trained though, right?"

"Yeah, but not as well as I need him to be. A couple of the guys have used him and done all right, won a few purses, but if he's going to replace Buster..." Brody shook his head.

Having watched her brother compete for years, she understood the kind of bond some men developed with their horses. She tilted her head and looked at Brody. She never would have expected him to be one of them, but obviously he was. Denise squeezed Brody's arm.

It took all of her concentration to focus on the horses instead of the man beside her. Geez, she'd need to get that under control if she had any hope of working with him. "Let's get him out of the trailer and go from there," she said then backed up to allow Brody room to maneuver the animal outside. "You can turn the other two loose in the other corral if you want, give them a little breathing room."

"Great, thanks."

* * * * *

An hour later Brody stood in awe, watching Denise put Rex through his paces. Somehow she was able to get Rex to do things Brody had never even known the horse could do, and she did it all with such ease. A softly spoken command, a gentle touch Rex immediately responded to. Rex was eating out of the palm of her hand. For some reason the horse was pulling out all the stops in an effort to please her.

Denise hopped down from Rex's back. She dug in her pocket and pulled something out then fed it to the horse. She gave his muzzle a quick pat and dropped her hands. Rex butted her with his head. Denise laughed. "Looking for a little more lovin' are ya? All right, baby," she cooed and stroked his nose.

Not liking being on the sidelines while Denise bonded with his horse, Brody joined them. "So what do you think?"

"He's great, so much potential for heading. He's strong, stops hard. He needs a little tweaking on the way he does a couple of things."

"Like?"

She turned her attention away from the horse and focused on him. "Who trained him?"

"Darby."

"That explains it," she murmured then turned back to Rex. She stroked the horse's nose and smiled sadly. "It might take a little getting used to, baby, but you are going to love working with me. My style is different, I promise," she whispered and kissed Rex's muzzle.

Brody watched her in confusion. She seemed to be communicating with the horse about something.

The horse flicked his head in agreement as if an understanding had been reached.

"That explains what? What do you do different?" Brody hated being in the dark. If there was something about Darby's training he needed to know then she'd damn well better tell him.

"Umm...let's just say Darby is a little more aggressive than I am in how he trains."

Brody's back stiffened. "What do you mean? Like he overworks the horse? Is there something wrong with Rex? Was he trained too young?"

"No, not that I know of. It's nothing like that."

"Then what?"

"Come on, Brody, you work around these guys, you know what some of them are like."

"I know Darby has a good reputation and his horses get the job done."

"Fine, then why did you come to me to work with Rex instead of taking him to Darby?"

Because despite Darby's track record with horses Brody thought he was a dick. The idea of not only forking over his hard-earned cash but spending time with the man as well set his teeth on edge. He looked at Denise and shrugged. "When Jus was on tour, he kicked my ass a few times and he gave all the credit to your horses so I thought I'd see what all the hype was about."

As difficult as it'd be to work with Denise and keep his hands to himself, it would be more than worth it if she was half as good as Justin had said. After watching her today, he wondered if maybe Justin hadn't downplayed just how good she really was. There was something about Denise that was truly special in the way she related to horses.

"All the hype?" She placed her hands on her hips and glared at him. "Hype implies I won't live up to expectations. Believe me, Brody, I'm better than you ever dreamed."

That's what I'm afraid of. "Prove it," he challenged.

"I plan to."

"Good, I'm looking forward to it."

What had she done? Agreeing to train Brody's horse was a great move professionally, but personally it was going to be a nightmare. Well she'd just have to put on her big-girl panties and suck it up.

She followed Brody into the sleeping area of the Featherlite. Looking around the space, she whistled. "Nice digs." She'd been in several of these types of trailers before but none of them had been as nice as this one.

"Thanks," he murmured. He pulled open the door of the fridge and eyed the contents inside. "I've got Coke or iced tea."

"Coke's good," she replied as she dropped down onto the sofa. She ran her hand along the leather. "This is nice. In Jus' trailer the sofa felt a little like a potato sack."

Brody laughed. "Yeah, well, your brother only stayed in his when he had to. I live in this one most of the time."

"What do you mean?"

"I don't really have a home base so this is it."

"How is that possible?" What kind of person didn't have a home base? She couldn't imagine not having someplace to go, a place where you belonged no matter what. She cocked her head to the side and examined Brody. She couldn't even begin to understand where he was coming from. Why didn't he want that?

"Most of the time when I'm not at a competition I just throw my trailer on Cord's property and make do," he told her.

"What does your roping partner's wife have to say about that?"

"She says eventually I need to grow up and buy a place of my own. She's just happy to have Cord home so he says she's fine with it because it keeps him home when we're training."

"So is that your game plan this year too? I'm not going to lie, Brod. It's going to take some doing to get Rex used to my style."

"What's so different about it?"

"I don't hit horses."

His brow wrinkled with confusion. "Neither do I."

Denise's jaw clenched as she remembered watching Darby take a stick to a horse when he'd thought no one was watching. "That's how Darby works. He has this theory about needing to show the horse who's boss. Hitting isn't my style." That was how her dad trained too, with a heavy hand and they'd never seen eye to eye on it.

Brody's knuckles clamped into a fist and turned white. Anger blazed behind his hazel eyes as he looked at her. "It's not my style either, so I think we'll be fine."

"That's good, but it's not going to be easy to get this done in the timeframe you have. If you want Rex to be ready for this season and be anywhere close to as in tune with you as Buster was, you're going to have to work with him a lot. I don't have the time to train him alone, so I'd need you to do a lot with him."

"No, that's great. I've got nowhere to be."

"So what? You'd park here?"

"Yeah, that was the plan."

Denise's shoulders straightened. "Little presumptuous, isn't it?"

"Not really. When I talked to Justin a couple of weeks ago, he was the one who suggested it."

"What?" Anger boiled inside her. How dare Justin make plans that involved her without asking? How many times had they fought about it over the years? She'd worked hard to prove herself as an equal on the ranch and he needed to treat her like a partner, not like his little sister.

"Shoot." Brody winced. "Can we pretend I didn't say that?"

Her spine stiffened. "No, we can't."

"Justin's going to kill me."

"What exactly did my brother say?" She was going to tear a strip off Justin when she saw him.

"He just said you were the best and if anyone could get Rex ready, it was you."

"And?"

"And, umm... When I asked about staying he said he didn't see why it would be a problem. He mentioned you were expanding the stables so you should have room to board the horses while we trained."

"Oh, he did, did he? And did he also discuss fees with you?"

"No...he said I'd have to talk to you about that."

"That was big of him," she growled.

"Can you maybe not mention to him that I told you?"

"Why? Did he tell you not to?"

"Uh..." He looked around the room and rubbed the back of his neck.

"Brody."

"Yeah, he might have said how you liked to be in control of your side of the business."

That was an understatement. She hated when anyone else got involved. She'd worked damn hard to build a name for herself and took pride in knowing she made all the decisions about the business.

Justin could have the ranch but this was hers. He knew she hated when he meddled, but somehow every now and then he couldn't stop himself from taking over. Guess she had her dad to thank for that. Growing up, they'd both had it hammered into them how useless women were. Honestly it was amazing that Justin re-spected her as much as he did. But every now and then that domineering side of his personality cracked to the forefront and her back immediately went up. The last thing she needed in her life was another man trying to control her. Been there, done that and had the scars to prove it.

It seemed the horse wasn't the only one who needed a little tune-up, but she'd deal with her brother later. "Fine, so Justin said you could squat on the property."

Brody winced. "Ouch, that's kind of harsh."

"Sorry," she mumbled. She wasn't really pissed at him, she was mad at her brother. And just because Brody had that same air about him didn't give her the right to attack him. "Let's try this again. So Justin said you could park here and we'd board your horses. What else did he say?"

"Nothing much. We both figured anything to do with training I'd need to discuss with you. Justin mentioned maybe you guys could use a hand while I was here, but nothing was firmed up."

Hmm, so her brother thought he'd be the one to reap some free labor, did he? Not going to happen. If she was the one boarding the horses and training them then she'd be the one to get paid—whether it was in cash or sweat equity, she didn't care. "Fine, it makes sense for you to earn your keep a bit. How are you with training cutters?"

"I can hold my own."

"Good, then when we're done with Rex for the day you can put in a couple of hours helping me with them."

"You've got a lot of them?"

"They're my bread and butter for now, so I have quite few that I work with at any given time."

"Sounds good to me. I'd be happy to help." Brody shifted on the sofa and curled his leg so he was facing her. His eyes roamed over her body.

Denise swallowed. Oh boy, she was definitely in trouble. She could barely keep her hormones in check being around him for a couple of hours. How was she possibly going to handle having him around for the next couple of months?

"So what's this going to cost me? Ballpark?"

Denise looked at him, so confident and in control. The real question was what would their arrangement cost her?

Chapter Three

Brody shifted in his seat Friday afternoon. He was exhausted. Denise hadn't been kidding he'd earn his keep working with her. He couldn't remember the last time he'd worked this hard. Not that he'd ever admit it to Denise, but the physical exertion had felt good. And he couldn't believe the progress in Rex already. If Rex kept responding as well as he was they stood a real chance of winning this year.

With his hat in his hand, he wiped sweat from his brow. Glancing around the corral, he spotted Justin leaning against the rail, watching them. Brody walked over and rested one hip against the rail, half watching Denise, half facing Justin. "What are you doing over here? Slacking off?"

"Nah, came over to talk to you actually. The guys and I are playing poker tonight if you want to join."

"What time?"

"Seven or so. It depends on what time my sister leaves."

"Where's Denise going?"

"I don't know. Out with the girls or something. No idea." He shrugged.

Relief swept through him. Girls' night, he could handle. The idea of Denise going out on a date made him want to punch something. Or someone.

He knew he had no claim on her but damn she got under his skin. She fought him tooth and nail on everything and for some perverse reason it turned him on even more. He normally went for the completely submissive type—buckle bunnies who fawned over him and did whatever he asked. He didn't really know what it was about Denise that made him want her so much. Maybe it was the challenge of getting her to submit to him. There was nothing sweeter than watching a strong woman being submissive. And Denise was stronger than most.

His eyes were drawn to her as she worked the horse around the corral. Whatever it was, there was no denying the fact he wanted her.

"So you in?" Justin's voice tore his attention off Denise.

"Yeah, sure," he mumbled.

"The horse looks good."

"He's coming along."

Denise lined Rex up in the box then burst forward and raced across the corral. "You weren't exaggerating when you said Dee was good."

"Told ya," Justin replied.

Brody couldn't take his eyes off her. She was so in command of everything she did. Denise never allowed anyone to see her not in complete control, which just made him want to see her surrender even more. His dick twitched and he stuck his hands in his pockets. Now was not the time to be thinking about this.

"I'll let you get back to it so my sister isn't the only one doing any work," Justin said and slapped Brody on the shoulder.

"Sure, see you tonight."

As Justin walked away, Brody stayed where he was and continued to watch Denise. He knew she wanted him, but for some reason she was fighting it every step of the way. He just needed to find out why so he could change her mind.

Denise rode up, stopped in front of him and dismounted. "All right, your turn. Let's see if you've been paying attention," she challenged.

Brody stepped forward and stopped in front of her. His body brushed against hers. "Believe me, I've been watching your every move."

Denise's eyes widened. Neither of them spoke as the air between them shimmered with awareness. He moved in closer, their bodies no longer just a whisper against each other but fully touching. Denise's breath hitched.

"You want me to tell you what I saw?" he asked.

She swallowed hard. "Sure."

"Watching you take that turn, I saw the way your legs flexed naturally to hold you in place and I wondered how they would feel wrapped around my waist," he whispered.

"Oh grow up." She smacked his arm and he stepped back, laughing.

He glanced down and saw her nipples poking through her shirt. She might not want to admit it but the idea turned her on.

He smirked at her. "You asked, darlin'."

"Not quite what I meant and you know it," she muttered.

"Maybe." He leaned in so his mouth was just about touching her ear and whispered, "But now I bet you're thinking about it too."

Not waiting for an answer, he turned and grabbed the reins of the horse. Unfortunately riding wasn't an option. He had to walk Rex over to the box since there was no way he was getting on the horse in his current state. It had been more than worth it to see the look on Denise's face. It wouldn't be long now. She was fighting it but she'd cave. He just needed to push her a little more.

How was she going to survive the next few weeks? They'd barely managed to make it through the first week and she was ready to give in. Her body was constantly aware of where Brody was at any given moment. When he gave her that look of his, she practically had to hold her panties up they were so eager to jump off on their own.

She needed to get her damn hormones under control. Guys like Brody were not right for her. He was too strong. Too controlling. Too everything. She'd get lost and become someone she didn't even recognize if she let herself. But lord, just looking at him she wanted to surrender everything and take him up on what he seemed to be offering. Frankly it pissed her off. She wasn't that girl. She'd worked too hard to prove she was an equal to any man to throw it all away because of a sexy swagger and great butt.

Annoyed with herself, she gripped her shovel harder. Cleaning out the stalls was never fun but being in the hot and sweaty confined space with Brody was almost unbearable. The way his muscles bunched up beneath his shirt, the flex of his shoulders. She sighed. The whole combination drew her attention like a moth to a flame. Denise dug her shovel into the dirty hay. If she just kept her hands busy then she wouldn't be so tempted to touch him.

"So I hear you're going out tonight. What are your plans?" Brody asked.

"Going dancing with the girls."

"Dancing, like at a bar with guys?" he growled.

"That's usually the best way to do it." She laughed. What the heck was his problem?

"Maybe you should stay home tonight."

"Yeah right, and watch you guys play poker? That sounds like a lot of fun."

"You could play."

"Nope, I'm not allowed. It's a guys-only game, no chicks," she scoffed.

Brody smirked. "Yeah, but we could use a beer girl."

She flicked her shovel and sent a load of soiled hay at his feet. "Dream on, buddy. I serve no man."

Brody looked up and stared at her. "Is that right?"

"That's right. I don't buy into that 'a woman's place is in the kitchen' bullshit."

"You don't cook?"

"Of course I do but not because it's my job. I take my turn like everyone else."

"Right."

Denise snorted and Brody raised his head. "What?"

"You probably like those women who live to serve their man, right?"

Brody shrugged. "There's definitely something to be said for a woman who wants to make her man happy."

"Yeah, right. You mean a woman who thinks you're God's gift."

"That too." Brody flashed his trademark grin. The sexy crooked smile graced posters that were hanging in girls' bedrooms all across America. There was a reason he was photographed so often and it wasn't just because of his track record. Brody Kyle was the perfect front man for the Pro Rodeo. Sexy and muscular with that cocky grin and the look in his eyes that said he could put those roping skills to work in the bedroom as well. And make you thankful he was doing it.

Well not her. She'd never let a man have that kind of control over her.

"What's the problem, Brody? You scared if you get a real woman with a mind of her own you won't measure up?"

"Measuring up's not going to be a problem, darlin'."

Denise snorted. "Is that what your groupies tell you?"

"I don't get any complaints, sugar."

"Of course not, because you pick women who think it's their job to just smile and look pretty and let the big, strong man take care of things for her." Denise batted her eyelashes. "Oh Brody, you're so strong, could you carry my bag for me? It's too heavy for little ol' me." She stuck out her lip in a mock pout. She'd seen the type of women he dated. The kind of girl who baby-talked and thought it was cute. It set her teeth on edge.

"There's nothing wrong with asking for help when you need it, Denise."

"Yeah, 'cuz that's what they're doing. God, men are so pathetic," she growled. "A woman pulls out that helpless routine and you all become idiots tripping over yourselves to be the big, strong man." She dug her shovel in so hard she slammed it into the ground, sending pain up her arms. Pissed off she was letting her emotions get the best of her. She glared at Brody. "That's not manly. You know what's manly? Manly is being able to accept a woman as your equal and being confident enough to be okay with that. Just because a woman is strong doesn't mean your masculinity's in question."

Angry, she shoveled faster. She needed to get this job done so she could get out of there. Being around Brody was hazardous to her health. The man was hot, but holy crap was he a pig.

"Keep it up, Denise." The warning tone in Brody's voice made her turn around.

"What?"

"You keep pushing me and I'm going to give you exactly what you're asking for."

She snorted. "Oh yeah, and what am I asking for, smart guy?"

"This," he muttered. He dropped his shovel and stalked toward her. The fire in his eyes told her she should retreat but she forced herself to stand her ground. She wouldn't give him, or any man, the satisfaction of seeing her back down.

He pressed her against the wall of the barn and gripped her wrists with his hands. He pushed her arms up above her head and manacled her there in his strong grip. Before she got a chance to speak, he crushed his lips against hers.

Who the hell did he think he was? Manhandling her like this. And damn it, what was wrong with her that she liked it? Sure she'd been secretly fantasizing about kissing Brody since she'd first met him. Yeah, her and every other girl.

She wanted him to kiss her out of passion, not anger. She bucked her hips to get him to move. He didn't budge so she did the only thing she could think of. She bit his lip.

He chuckled. Then the kiss changed. It was still dark and dangerous but now it was about seduction instead of anger. Lord help her, she wanted to fight his overbearing display but she found herself sinking into the kiss

Brody gripped both wrists with one hand, keeping her arms pinned above her head. He wrapped his free arm around her waist and pressed his hips into hers. She could feel his erection against her stomach. She groaned and arched her back into him.

God yes. This was what she'd been wanting all week—hell since the first time she'd laid eyes on him.

Surrendering to the moment, she closed her eyes and let her head fall back. Brody kissed and nipped at the soft skin on her neck. Goose bumps pooled on her skin. His tongue traced a path up her neck and he sucked her earlobe into his mouth.

"You might pretend you don't like it, Denise, but the idea of me taking control in the bedroom turns you on," he whispered into her ear.

His hot breath and the seductive words made her shiver. The arrogance of what he said pissed her off. "Fuck you. It does not," she growled.

He held her wrists tighter and pressed her against the wall. With his free hand, he stroked across her breast. Her nipple ached for more contact. Brody flicked the bud with his finger. "Well, your body says otherwise."

Her body betrayed her, responding to his touch. Humiliation swarmed through her. He was right. She did like the idea of submitting to a man in the bedroom and she hated that part of herself. She dropped her head forward. Brody's weight shifted and he tipped her face up with his hand. "Hey, what happened? One minute you were right there with me then the next..."

"Can you let me go, please?"

"Dee, what's going on? Talk to me."

"Brody, let me go, now."

He released her hands and backed away, putting some space between them. "Help me out here, Dee, what's going on?"

"I don't like to be manhandled," she grumbled, unable to meet his stare.

"Who was manhandling you?"

"What do you call it?"

"Intensifying things a little."

"A little...a little. Jesus, Brody, I-I..." she stammered. Her emotions were all over the place. She'd never felt anything like this before in her life. It was more than just kissing Brody. It was being controlled, not being able to move her hands. He scared her, but lord, he turned her on and that scared her more. She shook her head. "I can't do this. I've got to go."

"Denise, wait." He grabbed her wrist as she tried to push past. "What can't you do?"

"This." She waved her finger between the two of them. "This thing between us...I'm not that girl. I don't let guys control me. I don't do subservient."

Brody reared back as if he'd been hit. "Hold on, who asked you to be subservient?"

"You. That's the kind of women you go for. Where the hell have you been, Brody? That's what we were talking about."

"Yeah, sometimes that is the kind of woman I go for but believe me I'm very clear you aren't one of those women. Nothing about you says subservient."

"Well then what the hell was that about?"

His brow wrinkled as he looked at her. "Denise, there's a huge difference between being submissive and being subservient."

"Whatever," she mumbled. She couldn't do this. Being around him, knowing what it felt like to be in his arms—she ached to go back there and she couldn't allow herself to do that. She'd fought so hard to be independent, to be an equal to the men on the ranch. She wasn't about to just hand it all over because of one sexy guy.

She gave her arm a little tug and Brody released her. He looked confused and frustrated but she couldn't do anything about that. If she stayed she knew he'd kiss her again and if that happened all bets would be off.

"I gotta go," she told him and ran out of the barn. Outside she slumped against the wall. What did she do now?

Chapter Four

Brody threw his poker winnings on the dresser. Two hundred bucks. Not bad for a night with the boys. He sat and pulled off his boots then kicked off his jeans and underwear and threw them on the chair. Naked, he climbed into bed. He'd no sooner found a comfy position to sleep when a knock rattled the trailer door. Who the hell could that be? He pushed back the sheets and climbed off the bed. His feet hit the cold floor. The door rattled again.

"Hang on," he yelled. He didn't care who was at the door, he wasn't answering it naked. He grabbed his jeans off the chair and stepped into them, not bothering to do up the top button.

Stomping across the trailer, he muttered, "This better be good."

Brody threw open the door. His annoyance instantly turned to arousal when he saw Denise standing on his step. Her hair tumbled around her shoulders, looking sexy as sin. His eyes drifted down to the cleavage re-vealed by the low neck of her shirt. His mouth watered.

"So you gonna invite me in, cowboy?" she asked.

His body immediately reacted to the husky tone of her voice. "Uh, yeah, sure." He stepped back to allow Denise into the trailer. She tripped on the step and giggled then made her way inside.

Denise walked toward him. He couldn't take his eyes off the swing of her hips. Who was this woman? Denise didn't do the whole seductress thing so what was she doing?

"Dee, what's going on?"

She stopped in front of him and trailed her finger down his bare chest. "Isn't it obvious?"

His body certainly thought it was. He gritted his teeth to stop himself from grabbing her. This was Denise and he couldn't treat her like some bunny who'd showed up at his trailer in the middle of the night.

"Why don't you walk me through it?"

"Come on, Brody, you know why I'm here. Why does any woman show up at a man's place after a night out with the girls?"

"'Cuz she's horny."

"Bingo." She giggled and tapped his chest with her finger.

"Okay, but I thought you didn't want to go there with me."

"I think we both know I wanted to," she purred.

"Yeah, we did, but I need to listen to your mouth too."

Denise moved in closer to him. "Then listen to my mouth now. I want you."

His dick twitched. "You're drunk."

She rolled her eyes. "I'm not drunk. I've had a couple of drinks, that's all."

"Okay spell it out for me here, Denise. What do you really want?"

"I want you to do what you do."

"What I do?" He stuck his hands in his pockets to pull the fabric away from his body. His dick certainly knew exactly what it wanted.

"Mmm-hmm." She nodded.

"And what is it you think I do?"

"Come on, Brody. Don't make me explain it to you."

"No, Dee, I'm sorry, but I need to make you spell it out for me. I don't want to go into this thinking you're wanting one thing when really you're after something completely different."

Denise sighed. "I don't know. That's kind of the problem." She stepped away from him and dropped onto the couch, looking completely defeated.

What the hell was going on here? He knelt on the floor in front of her. "Dee, talk to me. What's going through that mind of yours?"

"I don't know. You make me want things, things I don't really understand."

"What kind of things?"

She worried her hands together in her lap and stared at them. "I don't know really, but in the barn, with you—" She sighed. "I felt things I've never felt before and I'm ashamed to admit it but I want more."

"Why are you ashamed to admit that?"

"Come on, Brody, look at me."

"I'm looking, believe me. I've been more than looking since the first time I saw you."

She glanced up at him. "What do you mean more than looking?"

"You have starred in some pretty heavy fantasies."

A slow smile spread across her face. Her nerves seemed to disappear, replaced by a confident, sexual woman. "Oh really?"

"Absolutely."

"What kinds of fantasies are we talking about?"

"I'm not sure you'd really be interested in hearing all of them."

"Try me."

He watched her, trying to weigh what she seemed to be telling him versus what would make her run in the other direction because the last thing he wanted to do was scare her away. But it wasn't as if he could hide who he was and what he liked in the bedroom. He was a take charge kind of guy, there was no hiding that. He was always going to need to be in control in the bedroom. He didn't know how to be any other way. Sure, he could do straight vanilla sex with no kink but the other part would always be there. He just wasn't sure how much she was willing to try to take on. And he didn't want to introduce too much too soon and scare her away. A woman like Denise was worth taking his time with. Building something. Not just running headfirst and scaring the crap out of her.

He'd wanted Denise for so long he didn't want to blow it. He knew he couldn't have her long-term. A woman like Denise would end up with a stable guy, one with roots, not a foster-home reject with nothing to his name but a fancy trailer and a couple of horses, but he wanted as much time with her as he could get. Already she mattered more to him than any other woman and he didn't want to mess that up by going too fast. But how much could she take before she started to get skittish?

"I'd love to tie your hands so you can't use them and have my way with you."

Denise's eyes widened.

Shit, had he gone too far? That was pretty tame compared to some of the things he wanted to do.

"My legs too?" she asked.

His dick throbbed against the fly of his jeans and he bit back a groan at the idea of Denise spread-eagle on his bed with her arms and legs tied. He cleared his throat. "Yeah, that would work."

"Okay," she whispered.

His head snapped up. There was no way he'd heard her right. "What?"

She chewed her lip and eyed him warily. "I'd like to try that."

He inhaled then slowly let the breath out. She was obviously new to this whole idea and as much as he wanted to rush headlong into this, he needed to take his time and make sure she was really comfortable with everything.

"You ever been tied up before?"

Denise shook her head.

"What have you done?"

She grimaced. "Normal stuff."

Normal stuff. He was pretty sure their definitions of normal varied greatly. "Has a guy ever pinned you down?"

She shook her head. "No, nobody has ever done anything like that until today in the barn with you."

"And you liked that?"

"Yeah." She chuckled. "It scares the shit out of me, but yeah, I really liked it. I haven't been able to think about anything else since this afternoon."

He took her hands between his and rested their clasped palms on her knees. "Why does it scare you?"

She shrugged. "I don't know. I've always been in control with everything. But today with you—" She took a deep breath. "I felt things I've never felt before and for whatever reason I really liked it and I shouldn't."

"Why? You like what you like, nothing wrong with that. We're both consenting adults."

"I know but..." She groaned. "I can't have it carry over out of the bedroom."

"Okay."

She cocked her head to the side and stared at him. "Okay?"

"Yeah, okay. You want to be able to submit in the bedroom but be your regular kickass controlling self everywhere else. That's fine, whatever."

"Seriously? You'd be fine with that?"

"Sure, why not?"

"Well because that's not how it works."

"What do you mean that's not how it works? This works however we say it does."

"Oh come on, Brody, I know how you guys operate. Hell, I've lived with guys like you all my life."

"What are you talking about? Justin sees you as an equal."

"Yeah, now he does, but I had to earn it."

"So? I've had to earn it too."

"It's not the same."

"Why?"

She rolled her eyes. "Only a man would say that."

If they went off on this tangent, there was no way he'd get her into bed tonight and he wasn't about to let that happen. "Look, Dee, we're getting off track here. You want to give up control only in the bedroom. I'm good with that. Screw what anybody else says. We make the rules for what happens between us. Okay?"

She nodded. "Okay."

"So is this a one-night thing?" he asked. Man, he sure hoped not. But if that was all she was offering he'd take it.

She chewed her lower lip and shook her head. "No, I don't want it just to be one night. I know you don't do relationships and all that, but if I'm doing this, if I'm going to allow myself to try this, I kind of want it to mean something."

Did this mean something? Working with her side by side every day, he'd gotten to know a different side of her. He respected her, honestly liked her as a person not just as a sexy woman he wanted to fuck. Already he was beginning to care about her. This wasn't just anonymous sex, this was Denise. So yeah, it would mean something. Shit, was he ready for that? He had to admit he kind of was.

She winced. "Shoot, that wasn't what I meant, I mean I know you don't do serious or anything but I sort of was thinking we could enjoy ourselves while you were here and if something continued after, great, but we'd keep it light. I'm not under any illusions that this means something to you or anything."

Brody rubbed the back of his neck. He didn't really like the picture she was painting of him. But he couldn't fault her for assuming he only did casual. Hell, normally the very idea of sex with emotion had him running for the hills. But with Denise he wanted that and here she was giving him the out. But would admitting that scare her away too? Crap, no wonder he avoided emotional involvement.

"So we'll keep things light and see where it leads us," he told her.

She smiled at him and nodded.

He leaned forward and placed a kiss against her lips. "Good. Now anything off-limits?"

"Umm." Her nose wrinkled up as she squinted. "My butt."

He coughed so he didn't laugh. "What do you mean your butt? Like don't touch it period or anal?"

She chewed her thumbnail nervously. "Anal."

Damn, he might have to work on that one with her but for now he was more than fine with tabling the discussion. "Okay, no problem. Anything else?"

"I'm not sure."

"That's fine, we'll go slow. I need a safe word for you so I know when you've had too much and you want to stop."

"You mean besides stop?"

"Well stop doesn't always mean stop now does it?" He winked at her.

She chewed on her lower lip as she watched him. "I guess not."

"Lots of people like to use the word red."

Her brows knit together in thought. "No, I don't want to use red." She tapped her finger against her lip thoughtfully. "Okay so a safe word. How about Ranger?"

He laughed. "Ranger, like your dog?"

"Yeah, he protects the house, makes me feel safe, it seems appropriate."

"All right, darlin', it's your safe word."

He pulled her to her feet. "Now that we've got the details out of the way we can enjoy ourselves."

When he pulled her close, he could smell alcohol on her breath. Shit, he was a jerk. He couldn't have sex with her when she was drunk and he was sober. What kind of asshole would he be? "You sure you haven't had too much to drink?"

"Do I seem drunk to you, Brody?"

"No, but I don't want to take advantage of you."

She licked her lips. "Oh honey, by all means take advantage."

Denise squealed as he swept her into his arms.

"My pleasure." He set her on the edge of the bed and slid her high-heeled shoes from her feet and kicked them out of the way.

He ran his hand up her jean-clad calf. He needed to see her naked. Now.

"Take off your shirt."

"What?"

"Take off your shirt."

She blinked. "Oh, okay." She slowly reached for the bottom of her shirt and pulled it over her head. Instead of tossing it to the side, she held it in front on her chest like a shield.

"You sure you want to do this, Dee?"

She looked down and nodded. "I'm sure."

He tipped her face up to look at him. Her blue eyes stormed. Arousal, confusion, surrender, they all warred with each other in the crystal depths. She wanted this but she hated that she did. He pressed a kiss to her lips, feeling hers soften beneath his as she gave in to the kiss.

As much as he wanted to live out the fantasy of Denise tied to his bed, he had the feeling if he pushed her too far too fast he'd completely blow it. The trick with Denise was to challenge her and to leave her wanting more. Normally he did everything full speed ahead, but normally he was just after a night of pleasure. With Dee, one night would not be enough. If he showed her all of him too soon, he was afraid he'd scare her off. This might be the time for patience rather than brute force. Seduction.

"Move your hands, darlin'."

She visibly swallowed, then dropped her hands onto the edge of the bed.

He traced his finger along the swell of her breast against the lace edge of her bra. He would have expected practical underwear from Denise but this whisper of blue silk and lace was anything but practical. Her nipples pressed against the fabric. He bent and sucked on the tight bud through the lace.

She inhaled roughly and arched her back toward him.

"Now the bra," he told her.

Denise's hands shook as she unhooked her bra and tossed it to the side.

"Gorgeous," he uttered. The nipple he'd sucked through her bra was a deeper red than the other one. The slight pressure had been enough to mark her pale skin. His cock throbbed against the fly of his jeans. He could already picture what her ass would look like with the mark of his hand. *Patience, Brod, go slow, this isn't a race, it's a journey.* If he played his cards right, she'd be willing to explore the endless possibilities between them.

"Now the pants."

She eyed him warily. "Are you just going to watch or are you going to lose yours too?"

He grinned. "Right now, I'm just enjoying the view."

"Oh, okay." She took a deep breath, stood and shimmied out of her jeans.

Holy hell, the panties matched the bra.

"Turn around."

She slowly spun so she was facing the bed. Damn, what was it about a thong? It was so much more than just having a naked ass on display. It was that tease of material between a woman's cheeks. He trailed his hand down her back and pushed her forward. With the raised platform, the bed was the perfect height to bend her over the mattress. He gripped her hips and pulled them back.

"Brody," she said nervously.

"Shh," he ordered and because he was unable to resist the temptation, he swatted her bare cheek. The pale skin pinkened up beautifully. He groaned. Taking things slow was going to be even harder than he'd imagined. He hooked his finger beneath the little slip of fabric and followed the line of elastic beneath her cheeks.

"Brody," she warned and tried to push off the bed.

He swatted her again. "Relax. I'm not going to do anything you don't want. You have to trust me if this is going to work, Dee. Do you trust me?"

She flopped back down on the mattress. "Yes," she whispered.

"Good." He rubbed his palm over her slightly pink cheek. "You've got an incredible body."

"Thank you."

Brody squatted so her ass was eye level. Pushing her legs apart, he could see the moisture from her pussy through the fabric of her panties. He inhaled deeply. Damn, she even smelled good. Cupping her ass in his hands, he nipped the bottom of her cheek and she squealed. Goose bumps danced across her skin.

He hooked his fingers in the edge of her panties and pulled them down her shapely thighs. Exposing her pussy fully to him for the first time. *Fuck me.* Brody bit back a groan.

Her pussy was neatly trimmed but not bare like most of the women he dated. He ran his finger through the short curls, making her groan. He grinned. A natural blonde.

Brody stood, gripped her hips and flipped her so she was lying on her back on the bed with her legs hanging off the edges.

He ran his hand up her calf. "So, Denise, what is it about being tied up that appeals to you? What turns you on more, the idea of your hands or your legs tied?"

He watched her as she struggled with what to say. He could see the war going on inside herself. "This doesn't work if you aren't truthful with me, honey."

"Okay." She nodded. "My legs," she whispered.

Legs, really? Interesting. He would have thought she'd say arms. "Legs. Why?"

She blushed and looked down, no longer making eye contact with him. "The idea of me being completely exposed to you, completely on display." She spoke so quietly he could barely hear her.

He leaned across the bed and tipped her chin up to look at him. "Good girl." He kissed her softly.

Standing back up, he glanced at the cupboard on his right. The toy chest. Would Denise freak out when she saw it? Probably, but oh well. He pulled open the cupboard and she gasped.

"Holy shit," she said. He looked at her. She didn't look horrified like he'd expected. If anything, she looked intrigued and a hell of a lot more aroused. This was turning out even better than he could have imagined.

He withdrew two lengths of rope from the cupboard and shut the door. Grabbing Denise's hips, he slid her forward on the mattress so her ass was at the edge of the bed, putting her pussy fully on display. He formed a loop in one end of the rope and hooked it around Denise's ankle then threaded it through the hook on the top of the wall, pulling her leg up and to the side.

"Oh wow, umm..." Denise stammered.

"You okay?"

She nodded. "Yeah, I just hadn't pictured my legs up in the air but..." She sighed. "N-no," she stuttered. "I'm good, carry on."

Denise's breathing hitched as she watched him. He could see the moisture dripping out of her pussy already.

He stroked her leg. She was so nervous, but so brave at the same time. The contrast was incredibly sexy. He couldn't remember ever wanting a woman as much as he wanted Dee.

He hooked the other rope around her left ankle and tied it to the second hook in the ceiling.

With her legs up in the air and her pussy completely on display she looked incredible. This position would make her pussy so tight around his cock. He couldn't wait to bury himself inside her.

"You okay?" he asked as he dragged a finger through her drenched slit.

Denise moaned. "Yep, this definitely works."

He grinned at her. "It absolutely works. You look hot as hell." His cock ached behind the fly of his jeans. He shifted the material and it just pinched more. Ah, screw it. He kicked off his jeans and left them on the floor. Unrestricted, he knelt down, placing her pussy at eye level.

His first taste of her was pure, liquid sin. Her musky flavor coated his tongue, spicy and sweet and so uniquely Dee. Wanting to taste more of her, he pressed his tongue inside her hot pussy.

"Yes," she hissed.

He fucked her with his tongue a couple of times, enjoying the way her tight pussy clamped around his tongue. He could only imagine how good it would feel around his cock. Replacing his tongue with his finger, he moved it back and forth while he swirled his tongue around her clit. Denise's hand threaded through his hair.

He had to admit, as much as he liked tying a woman up there was something incredibly hot about having her pull on his hair in the throes of passion.

Needing to feel her release, he drove her higher, swirling and sucking her clit into his mouth. Her nails dug into his scalp as she tried to hold him closer to her body.

He crooked his finger forward and rubbed against her G-spot. "Oh god, Brody," she gasped. "What the hell was that?"

"Just enjoy," he murmured against her.

Denise's pussy clenched around his finger, she was close already. He took her clit lightly between his teeth. Some women liked the little bite of pain while others hated it. As he bit down a little more, Denise moaned and bucked her hips forward. Guess she was one of the ones who liked it. He pressed harder and she exploded around him. Her pussy squeezed his finger tightly as she came.

His dick was rock hard when he stood. He grabbed the condom he'd set on the edge of the bed and put it on. Denise watched him, her eyes wild with hunger.

He placed himself at the entrance to her pussy and drove home in one deep thrust. Denise moaned. Her nipples tightened further into hard pebbles of arousal.

"Please, Brody, fuck me," she pleaded.

Gripping her hips with his hands, he drove into her. Her pussy was so tight he wasn't going to last long. He started off slow, enjoying the way she gripped his shaft. The little mewing sounds she made were driving him crazy. Even with her legs tied, she tried to buck toward him, meeting him thrust for thrust. He held her hips firmly, anchoring her to the bed as he drove hard and deep into her. Denise moaned loudly and her back arched off the bed. Her pussy clamped around his cock as she came.

Her surrender increased the need driving through him. The muscles in his back flexed as his balls drew up tight against him. The orgasm slammed through him, draining the blood from his head as everything fired to his cock. He jerked as he came. Leaning against Denise, he tried to catch his breath. Holy hell.

He looked at her. She lay with her arm over her eyes, her body completely lax against the mattress as her chest rose visibly with each breath.

Forcing himself from her hot body, he stepped back. Denise opened her eyes and watched him. He discarded the condom then returned and set about unhooking her legs.

She groaned as she stretched out the first freed leg while he released the other. Once her limbs were untied, he gripped her around the waist and eased her up onto the bed properly with the pillow beneath her head. Sitting on his knees, he massaged her right calf then slowly worked up her leg. Denise moaned in pleasure. "Oh that feels amazing."

"You okay?"

She smiled at him. "I'm more than okay."

He moved over to her left leg and gave it a quick rubdown as well to ease any knots she might have from being tied for so long. He hadn't meant to work her that hard the first time, but she'd responded so eagerly, as if she'd been craving this her entire life. He lay down beside her and eased his arm under her head.

Denise curled into him, resting her head on his chest. "That was amazing," she murmured.

"Good."

"I can't believe you have a hook in your ceiling for sex."

He laughed. "There are hooks in the head and foot-boards too," he told her.

She sat up and squinted at the headboard. "Where?"

"See the funny knot design?"

"Yeah," she replied.

"If you push it, they pop out so you can thread a rope or handcuffs through them, the same ones are at the foot."

She lay back down and placed her head on his chest. "Wow, I can't believe they put that kind of thing in a trailer. Is that what those are supposed to be used for?"

"Mmm-hmm, a friend of mine did the design and I had it custom made for the bed." He hooked his fingers into her hair and let the silky strands slide across his palms.

"Geez, I really have led a sheltered life," she murmured.

He chuckled. "Don't worry, I plan to do my best to remedy that."

She tilted her head and looked up at him. Her full lips curled into a luscious smile. "Good, because I'm eager to learn."

With a growl, he flipped on top of her and pinned her beneath him. No time like the present.

Chapter Five

The following morning, Denise rolled over and looked at the empty space beside her in her bed. She wished she'd been able to stay with Brody all night but that would have brought up way too many questions and she wasn't ready to deal with the inquisition from her brother and friends over breakfast just yet. She was having a hard enough time dealing with what she was feeling on her own without those three weighing in.

Had Brody been telling the truth? Would he be able to handle her being the boss when it came to training after she'd handed him control over her body? She prayed he was.

Last night had been the most liberating sexual experience of her life. With her previous boyfriends, they'd been pleasers, always checking with her to make sure she liked what they were doing. It had always been pleasant, but wow, having a man just take control was on a whole other playing field. She wasn't sure it was even the same game. Brody had done things to her and taken her to heights she hadn't known existed.

Her stomach flipped at the idea of seeing him again this morning. She sighed and pushed herself off the bed. She couldn't wait any longer.

She quickly threw on her jeans and shirt then braided her hair into one long tail. Her hand strayed to her makeup and she fought the urge to primp and fuss over her appearance. She took two steps toward the door then turned around and grabbed her mascara off the dresser. Mascara wasn't really makeup, it was a staple, like sunscreen, and just because she didn't wear either every day didn't mean she shouldn't. *Yeah right.*

Denise wandered down the hallway and could hear the guys talking over breakfast. She looked at Duncan and Kasey and shook her head. "I thought when you were promoted to foreman you were going to stop mooching breakfast off me on the weekends because you had your own kitchen." She put her hands on her hips and stared at the two men. "I know Shelly told me she stocked your fridge."

Denise didn't know what they were going to do when Shelly retired at the end of the summer. Finding someone willing to cook for the ranch hands wasn't going to be an easy chore. Shelly and Jimmy had been working on the ranch for as long as Denise could remember. When Jimmy had retired this fall, it had hit them all hard.

Thank goodness Duncan had stepped easily into the foreman role. Unfortunately, it wasn't going to be easy to replace their cook. Not many people were willing to put up with the shenanigans of feeding a bunch of hungry ranch hands three squares a day, which is why they gave Shelly the weekends off, to keep her sane.

Duncan stood and rounded the table with his coffee mug in hand. He paused beside her. "You'd miss me too much if you didn't see me. Besides, what kind of weekend would it be if I had to start my day without breakfast with a beautiful woman?" He kissed her cheek then wandered over to the coffeepot. He pulled a second mug out of the cupboard, filled it up and doctored it the way she liked it then handed it to her.

"Thanks, Dunc."

"No problem."

Denise eyed her brother as he flipped pancakes with a smile on his face. "You look like you won at poker last night."

Justin blinked a couple of times as if he just realized she was in the room then he laughed. "No, got my ass handed to me at the table last night."

"By who?"

"Brody was the big winner. He took us all for a ride."

Denise snickered. He'd more than taken her for a ride, that was for sure.

"What are you laughing about?" Justin asked. "I thought my sister was supposed to cheer for me."

"I do, don't worry," she placated. "So if you lost at cards how come you're smiling so big this morning?"

"Kat called last night. Her final assignment is a road trip, which she can email back to the magazine, so she's ready to move out now rather than at the end of the month."

"That's awesome, Justin."

Justin stood watching her. "So umm...that's the other thing I need to talk to you about."

Denise's stomach twisted into a knot. That was three weeks early. Her place would never be ready by then. When she'd been given her own corner of the ranch for her facility, she'd always planned on building her own house there. And when Justin and Kat got together it made sense for her to finally act on her plans. Having Kat move to Arizona had taken a someday dream and brought it to the forefront. The last thing she wanted was to live with the happy couple full time. It was bad enough living together for short periods of time. Couples definitely need their own space. As much as she loved Kat and was thrilled for her brother, she'd been hoping to be in her own place by the time Kat moved in or at least within a couple of weeks.

When she'd talked to the head guy on the job site mid-week, he'd thought they were about three to four weeks out, which meant she'd be living with the happy couple for almost a month now. Not good.

"Kat wants me to fly out there this weekend and drive back with her. We'll hit the spots she needs to visit on the way here, so I'll be gone about two weeks."

"Two weeks?" Her jaw dropped. Ever since Justin had quit the rodeo tour he hated being gone from the ranch for longer than an overnight trip. Two weeks. Wow, guess it was true about the things people did for love.

"Yeah, but don't worry. I already talked to the guys and Kasey and Dunc are cool with it and Brody said he could lend a hand if needed so I'm covered. It won't be any extra work for you."

"I wasn't worried about that," she told him. She'd been expecting him to ask her to move into her own place early.

"What was the face for then?"

"Nothing really. I was just thinking I could move into the foreman's place with Duncan and Kasey if you want when Kat gets here." She turned to the other two men. "You guys aren't using the third bedroom are you?"

Kasey's eyes widened and Duncan started to laugh. "Nope, third bedroom isn't being used."

"Second either," Justin mumbled.

What the hell was that about? Of course, they were using the second bedroom. That didn't even make sense.

Justin snickered as he looked at his friends then turned back to her. "Don't be ridiculous. This is just as much your place as mine. Kat and I are fine with you staying here."

She glanced over at Kasey as he visibly relaxed into his chair. Ouch, that hurt. Why didn't they want to live with her? "I wouldn't be that bad of a roommate," she muttered.

"What?" Kasey asked. Then he groaned. "No, Dee, of course you're more than welcome to move in with us if you want to. It's not that at all, honest."

"Gee thanks." She grabbed the plate of pancakes Justin slid toward her and sat. She liberally poured syrup all over the stack and had just shoved a big bite into her mouth when she heard the back door slam shut. She looked up with her mouth full and nearly choked. Brody. His eyes homed in on her and her body instantly reacted. A shiver ran through her and she gasped, sucking in the mouthful of pancake. Oh crap, she thought a moment before she started coughing.

Kasey and Duncan pushed up from the table, Brody and Justin both rushed toward her and she waved all four men off.

The coughing fit that ensued put away any hope she had of remaining cool when she saw him. Somehow coughing pancake across the table just didn't lend itself to keeping up the illusion of being sexy. She dropped her head onto the table. *Lord, just shoot me now.*

A hand touched her shoulder. She glanced up to find Brody staring at her with his brow knit with concern. There was no way she could salvage this with her dignity, so she went for amusing instead.

"The pancakes are so good I almost died. You should try some."

He laughed. "You sure you're okay?"

"Of course." She waved her hand as if she nearly choked to death every day.

"Maybe if you ate like a lady instead of trying to beat Dunc in how many pancakes you can shove in your face at one time that wouldn't happen," Justin told her.

This was mortifying. She could only imagine what Brody was thinking of her. Too afraid to look at him, she glanced up to see Duncan watching her. He winked. She grinned back and they both flipped Justin the finger without looking at him.

Brody burst out laughing and squeezed her shoulder. "You really are one in a million, Dee," he said then kissed the top of her head. Her eyes bugged out. She could feel Justin, Duncan and Kasey all watching her.

Act cool, she told herself. She smiled at Brody. "Do you want some coffee?"

"Yeah, sure, that would be great. Can I top anyone up?"

Inside Denise did a little jig. He hadn't asked her to get his coffee for him. Holy cow maybe he'd been serious about the bedroom being an island unto itself where anything goes. "Yes, please," she replied.

He grabbed her cup then walked over to the coffeepot. She went back to eating her breakfast without looking at the guys.

"If you want some pancakes I'm sure Justin has lots," she called to Brody.

"Thanks, I'm good. I ate before I came over," Brody replied as he made his way back to the table with two mugs in his hands. He deposited hers then took the chair beside her.

Justin set his plate down heavily on the table, drawing everyone's eyes to him as he sat. He rested his elbows on the table and sneered at Brody. "Is there something you need to tell me?"

"No, there isn't," Denise replied.

"If he's involved with you then yeah he does need to tell me."

"Oh and why's that?" Denise demanded.

Brody put his hand on her arm. "It's fine," he told her then turned to look at the three men across the table from them. "I get it, all three of you have made it perfectly clear what'll happen if I hurt Dee, but honestly, guys, it's not your call whether we get involved or not. The only person whose opinion matters on the subject is Denise. End of discussion. I know you all respect her judgment so continue to respect it, because right now I'm not the one hurting her. You all are." With that Brody stood and held out his hand to her. Denise's heart fluttered. Wow.

She took Brody's hand and followed him outside. Normally having someone speak for her would have driven her crazy, but for some reason it didn't seem like that was what Brody had done. No one had ever stood up to her brother for her, let alone standing up to Duncan and Kasey too. For the first time in her life she actually felt like the guy she was interested in understood her.

"Thank you," she told him.

He wrapped his arms around her and kissed the top of her head. "Sorry I jumped in. I know you could have handled it but they were pissing me off."

She laughed. "I know the feeling. You get used to it."

Brody leaned back and tilted her chin up with his finger. "I can't promise I won't hurt you, Denise."

"I'm not asking you to. I'm a big girl, Brody. I can handle it."

His eyes darkened as he watched her. "I have no doubt you can."

She licked her lips, enjoying the way Brody tracked the movement with his eyes. "What did you have planned for today?" she asked and rubbed her breasts against his hard chest. Maybe she could convince him to spend the day in bed.

"That's not how it works."

"How what works?" she asked coyly and trailed her hands down the muscles in his back.

"Nice try." He tapped her nose then stepped away from her. "Why don't you show me this house of yours you've been talking about? Then we can get some train-ing in this afternoon with Rex."

"What?" He couldn't be serious. She'd laid sex on the table and he was denying her. What was wrong with him? What guy in his right mind did that?

"Your house. I want to see it."

She stared at him with her mouth gaping. She didn't think she was that out of practice in the art of seduction. Hell, it had worked pretty good last night. She stepped closer to him. "I'm pretty sure we'd have more fun if we stuck around here."

"Trust me, darlin', we'll have plenty of fun, but remem-ber I'm running the show." Moisture pooled in her core as she remembered the way he'd controlled her the night before.

"Fine, we'll play it your way," she mumbled.

Brody chucked. "Don't pretend you didn't love every minute of it."

She wrinkled her nose at him. "You don't have to be a jerk and rub it in, though," she grumbled.

He cupped the back of her neck. "Rubbing it in implies I think it's bad you like it and that couldn't be further from the truth."

His finger stroked her skin and she shivered beneath his touch. Why did she react to him this way? No other guy had ever set her off so quickly with a single touch.

Brody bent and took her lips with his. Firm, demand-ing. Helpless, she fell into the kiss, her mouth opening of its own volition for his tongue to sweep inside. Her legs trembled and she leaned against him. She wrapped her arms around his waist and held on. Brody slid his thigh between her legs, the hard muscle brushed against her sensitive clit through her jeans and she moaned.

He threaded his hand through her hair and pulled her head back. Arousal shot through her, soaking her panties. She arched her back, trying to press her body against him.

His nostrils flared as he stared at her. "Not yet, little one. You need to learn some patience."

"I don't want to be patient. I want you now," she groaned.

"That's why you'll wait. You need to learn to deny yourself pleasure." He nipped her bottom lip. "It'll make the release when you submit that much better."

"I think the release would be pretty fantastic now."

He swatted her ass. "Patience or you'll pay the price."

Her pussy clenched with need at the domineering tone of his voice and the promise of how he could control her body.

A slow, carnal smile spread across Brody's face. "Maybe you like the idea of being punished." He pulled her hair harder. The pain in her scalp felt as if it was directly tied to her clit. She wanted him, wanted him to take her, to demand what he wanted, to use her. This wasn't right. She should be ashamed of herself for wanting that but she wasn't. Instead she was completely turned-on.

"Interesting," Brody murmured as he continued to watch her.

Could he really read her so easily? The look in his eyes said he could. She licked her lips. Was she ready for what he had to offer? He moved his thigh between her legs and rubbed against her clit. She closed her eyes. God, yes, she was more than ready, she needed this.

She ground against Brody's thigh. The firm pressure hit her exactly right. He pinched her nipple and she gasped. Lord, she was practically humping his leg. She knew she should stop but she was so close. Just a little more.

Suddenly Brody pulled his leg away from her. *No, no, no.* "What are you doing?" she cried.

"I told you, I'm calling the shots and you're going to wait until I'm ready to let you come. And I'm not done playing yet."

Chapter Six

During the short drive over to her new place Brody had teased her relentlessly. Her panties were soaked. She looked over at him and scowled. The jerk just winked back. Frustrating man.

They exited the truck and Denise looked up at the outside of her new home. It was all hers. Well, hers and the bank's. The outside was completely finished and looked exactly how she'd imagined.

A whistle off to the side drew her attention to Brody. "Very nice."

Pride swelled through her. "Thanks, I like it." It was strange how much she wanted Brody to like what she'd done.

She led the way inside. The front entrance area opened into the main hallway. A few short steps and off to the left it opened up to where her main living area with open kitchen would be. The plumbing was all roughed in and the drywall was up and the first coat of paint was on some of the walls. Once the painting was all done this week then the floors would go in. She could already picture how amazing it would all look when the hardwood floors went in.

Brody brushed up behind her. He was so close she could feel his breath against her neck. She shivered. Waiting was torture. It was official she was not cut out for patience when it came to orgasms.

"So give me the grand tour," Brody told her.

Well she'd show him. This was her pride and joy. She could talk about it all day. By the time they were done he'd be begging her to stop talking so they could have sex. She smirked to herself as she led Brody into the living room. *Patience my ass.* It was all about perspective.

A big window covered one wall, giving her a clear view of the mountains.

"Nice view," Brody commented.

"Mmm, I know. That's why I positioned the house this way. I wanted to be able to sit on my porch or sit in here and see the mountains."

"It must be nice to know this is all yours." His voice sounded wistful as he looked out the window at the mountains.

In some ways he was still such a mystery to her. She couldn't imagine living out of a trailer all year 'round. "Yeah it is. What about you? You ever wanted to lay down roots someplace, have a home base?"

He shrugged. "Sure, who hasn't?"

"So what's stopping you?"

"I don't know, time maybe." He stuck his hands in his pockets and looked down at the ground. "Honestly,

I'm not sure I'd even know how to go about building a home."

"What do you mean?" How could he not know? With his attention to detail and the way he wanted everything just right, he could create a great home.

He laughed but the sound held no humor. "I don't know. I've never really had one so I don't have a lot to go on. All I know is what I don't want. I haven't really given much thought to what I do." He looked around. "But this...what you're building here, you and Justin, it's pretty damn amazing." He nodded. "Yeah, something like this would be..." He left the words hanging in the air.

Gone was the confident guy she was used to, in its place was a vulnerability she never would have expected Brody to show her. Her heart squeezed tightly. Damn, the confident Brody was hard enough to resist but seeing how deeply he cared just made him that much more appealing. There was so much more to Brody than she'd ever imagined. She found herself wanting to know everything about him. What had put that look on his face or the sadness she sometimes saw in his eyes?

"Why don't you buy a place and set down some roots?"

"I'm not even thinking about that until I have enough money in the bank to pay for something outright."

Confused, Denise wrinkled her nose. With all the endorsements Brody had there was no way a bank wouldn't give him a loan for a place. "That's what banks are for."

Brody snorted. "Yeah, no. I know how banks work. I'm not borrowing money for anything. If I can't afford to buy it and maintain it on my own then I'm not going to buy it."

"Why? You could just borrow some money and be in a place of your own sooner."

"And run the risk of having it taken away from me? No thanks." He shook his head. "When I get my own place, it's going to be mine."

The determination in his voice surprised her and she longed to know what had happened in his past to make him so adamant on the subject. "Why would it be taken from you?"

Brody ran a hand through his hair. "Do we really need to talk about this?"

She placed her hand on his arm. "Yeah, I think we do."

He exhaled audibly. "Fine. The thing is rodeoing is dangerous. One good injury and I'm done. No more endorsements, no money, nothing. I'm not prepared to buy something that I can't afford to maintain on my own when the endorsements dry up." He looked out the window. "Geez, I can only imagine how much it costs to run a place like this." His head slowly bobbed up and down as he stared out at the yard. "Something like you've got here, that's worth holding on to forever."

She studied Brody. There was so much more going on than what he was telling her. She sighed. Baby steps. He'd opened up this much, maybe eventually he'd trust her enough to tell her the rest. She really hoped so. Brody didn't trust easily, he didn't lean on anyone. And she realized how much she wanted to be that person for him. She just needed to be patient.

When she'd first met Brody, he seemed like this aloof, good-time guy, but now she knew that wasn't at all who he was. Every time she turned around she discovered new things about him. New reasons to like him.

She chewed on her bottom lip. This was supposed to be light and fun, simple, just sex. And as much as that wasn't quite what she wanted anymore that's what they'd agreed on. She needed to remember that and keep it light.

"Come on, check this out," she said. Grabbing his hand, she pulled him toward where her kitchen would be. She stopped at the kitchen window and stared out at the corrals and stables. A slow smile spread across her face, pride filled her as she looked at what she had built. The business her father had thought was destined to fail had become a bigger success than anyone had ever imagined. Who would have thought she'd be expanding her own facility already?

The expansion on the stables had been completed several months ago but she hadn't been using it yet. She'd moved her training over to the old corrals, closer to the main house, during construction, so the horses didn't get spooked by all the noise. It was hard enough to train some of the horses without adding the sound of nail guns firing intermittently throughout the session. Now the exterior was finished and assuming nothing unforeseen popped up she should be able to move all the animals back over within the next couple of days.

Brody wrapped his arms around her waist. "Looks like some setup."

She leaned back against him. "Yeah it's going to be amazing. It turned out better than I imagined."

"I didn't even realize you had all this back here. Why haven't we been using it?"

"We will, starting this week."

"Can't wait."

The air in the room changed. The sadness she'd felt a few minutes ago from Brody was gone, making her wonder if she'd imagined it.

He leaned in close. His hard cock brushed against her spine as he pushed her braid over her shoulder and kissed the side of her neck.

Denise shivered and tilted her head to give him better access.

Instead of continuing, Brody stopped and stepped away from her.

Confused, she spun around to face him.

"Take off your shirt."

"What?"

"I said take off your shirt." He leaned against the wall and crossed his arms over his chest. Powerful, commanding.

She swallowed at the heat she saw in his eyes. There was no question he wanted her as much as she wanted him but if that was the case then why hadn't he just taken her up on her offer at the house?

"I'm waiting, Denise. Don't make me take it off for you."

"Oh yeah, what's going to happen if you do?"

His posture changed, like a predator stalking a weaker prey. He took a step toward her. "I'll bend you over the saw horse and tan your ass."

"You wouldn't dare," she said. She bristled at the implication. She was a grown woman. He wasn't going to spank her like a petulant child. But even as the thought ran through her, excitement warred with outrage. What was wrong with her? How could the idea excite her? What had he done to her?

"Wouldn't I?" He stalked toward her.

"Don't even think about it, cowboy." She backed away from him. Excitement, fear, arousal. They all warred inside her at the heated look on Brody's face.

"Take off your shirt."

From somewhere inside came the need to push him, to challenge him to do what he threatened. "Make me." Excitement zipped through her, moisture pooled in her core as she tried to dart past him.

With lightning speed, he grabbed the front of her shirt. He hooked his hands in the fabric and ripped her shirt open, sending buttons flying across the floor.

Denise gasped. Holy shit, that was hot.

His eyes narrowed as he stared at her. "You can take the pants off on your own or I'll give them the same treatment as your shirt," he rasped. The look on his face told her he wasn't kidding.

She squeezed her legs together and shifted to ease the ache in her pussy.

"Now, Denise," he ordered.

Slowly, she lowered her jeans to the floor and stepped out of them. He grabbed the edges of her button-down shirt and pushed it off her shoulders. Instead of taking it off her arms, he pulled the fabric so her wrists were trapped behind her back in the material. The shirt was as effective as any handcuffs in securing her.

She squirmed beneath his scrutiny. What did he have planned next?

He led her to the sawhorses and the makeshift table. He peeled his shirt off and lay it down across the wood like a blanket. Pressing his hand in the small of her back, he said, "Lie down."

Denise glanced over her shoulder at him. Unease drifted up her spine. Damn, what had she asked for? "Umm," she stammered.

"Lie down." The calluses on his palm brushed across her back and she shivered.

"Yes sir," she murmured and raised her hand to her forehead as she gave him a sarcastic mock salute.

"Sir, I like that," he replied.

Denise rolled her eyes. Of course, he liked it. Typical.

But if he liked it and she played along, maybe he'd go easy on her. She took one last look at him then did as she was told. The wood was hard beneath her chest. Nerves battled with arousal. The combination was a heady jolt to her system. She didn't know if she should turn and flee or close her eyes and enjoy.

He peeled her panties down her legs then kicked her feet apart, spreading her legs wide. Brody swept a finger through her pussy. "You're drenched."

He firmly rubbed against her clit. She could feel it swell beneath his touch. She closed her eyes. Brody plunged two fingers inside her and she moaned.

"Oh no, you're not getting off that easy." He ran his hand down her back then rubbed his rough palm against her cheeks. "I think ten strokes will do the trick to teach you not to disobey me."

"Ten?" she asked, outraged. He had to be freakin' kidding if he thought she was going to let him whack her ten times.

"Should we make it more?"

"No," she grumbled. What if it hurt? What if she didn't like it? Would he stop? Her nipples painfully dug into the wood as arousal surged through her. What if she did like it? How could she be this turned-on just thinking about being spanked? She was a freak. *A hugely aroused freak.*

"Count them."

God, this was humiliating and yet somehow it just made the whole thing that much more arousing.

He thrust his finger into her. She pressed back, trying to arch her back. The first smack against her bare ass made her groan.

"Out loud."

"One." She should tell him to stop but she couldn't. The desire to play this out and see where he took her was stronger than her fear of the unknown. If the next nine felt anything like the first stroke, she was going to be screaming in pleasure when he was done. She needed to find out.

He teased his finger around her clit. Her entire body quivered with need. She was so close already.

The second swat was considerably harder than the first. The pain in her ass was in direct contrast with the pleasure in her clit, intensifying both. She pressed her hips back. He continued to spank her as she counted out loud. With each hit, he tormented her pussy with his fingers, driving her to the edge of control. She squirmed on the table.

"Don't come," he demanded.

"What?"

"Don't orgasm, Denise. I told you, you have to earn it."

Sadistic bastard. Her skin was on fire, her pussy ached. The combination was almost more than she could bear.

He flicked her clit and she had to grit her teeth as the orgasm threatened to overtake her. "Eight," she said through gritted teeth.

Nine hit hard, tears formed in her eyes. The need to come was so strong. She didn't think she could take it. What would he do if she orgasmed when he'd told her not to?

She loved it and hated it. This wasn't who she was, and yet it absolutely was exactly what she'd been missing.

Finally ten landed against her ass. She groaned and he drove his finger into her pussy. It was too much, her senses felt completely overloaded.

She heard the crinkle of a condom wrapper. Her heart raced. Oh thank god, he was going to fuck her.

He gripped her hips and thrust into her deep and hard. She arched her back and pressed into him. "Yes," she hissed.

He thrust into her slow, then fast, alternating the pace, keeping her completely on edge so she never knew what was coming next. The man completely overwhelmed her. She gasped for air. It was too much.

Brody reached around her and flicked her clit. She closed her eyes tightly as white light flashed behind her eyelids. The orgasm that tore through her made her scream with ecstasy. She lay limp on the table as Brody thrust into her once, twice, and then his body went rigid behind her as he groaned out his own orgasm.

He leaned against her back and nipped her earlobe, sending a shiver down her spine. "Not much of a punishment when you enjoy yourself that much, darlin'."

"I didn't enjoy it."

He chuckled. "Bullshit."

Okay, he was right, but she didn't want to have enjoyed it.

Brody pulled away from her to dispose of the condom. He returned a second later. He sat down on the edge of the makeshift table, picked her up and cuddled her. She inhaled deeply. He smelled like soap, sex and Brody. She sighed and snuggled deeper.

"You doing okay, darlin'?" he asked and kissed the top of her head.

"Never better," she murmured and she realized it was true. Oddly enough, she didn't feel ashamed about what had happened between them. Sure it had been a little weird during, but now lying here with Brody it felt fine. No shame. He made it all seem so normal. Like anything that happened between them was cool and nothing to be embarrassed about. She hadn't known that was possible.

Brody made her feel better than she could ever remember. Hell, for the first time in her life she felt like someone really understood her. He respected her and listened to her as an equal on the ranch. He made her feel important. And somehow in the bedroom, he'd given her something she hadn't even known she'd been missing. She sighed. It was official. She was crazy about him. So much for keeping things simple.

The following morning, Denise wandered out to the stables. Brody had spent several hours in her bed but when it came time to sleep he'd moved to his trailer. As much as she wanted him to stay, she wasn't about to beg him, there were some lines she wasn't ready to cross. It was one thing to beg him for an orgasm. It was another to beg a guy to stick around afterward, especially a guy like Brody who never stuck around anywhere for very long. Just because what they had wasn't a one-night stand didn't mean it mattered to him more than one. Everyone knew he didn't do commitment.

She needed to be smart and remember she was just another stop on the rodeo tour like every other woman he'd been with. And her head needed to remember that, because her stupid heart was starting to believe otherwise. Thank goodness she'd always prided herself on leading with her brain, not her heart.

Heading out to the barn, she paused and tilted her head back to feel the sun on her face. There was still a chill in the air, making the first rays of sun feel even better. Birds chirped around her. Soon the sounds were echoed by more birds as if they were calling each other to say come out and enjoy the sun too.

When she opened her eyes, she saw Brody leaning against the barn door, watching her. Self-conscious, she brought her hand up to her hair to make sure it was all in place. Silly really since she'd just done her hair, but she wanted to look good for him.

She took a deep breath and strolled toward him.

"Morning," she said.

"Morning." His eyes roamed over her body like a caress. Her nipples instantly jumped to attention.

"You ready to move the horses?"

"You bet." He nodded. "Is it just you and me, or is anyone else helping?"

"No, Kasey and Duncan said they'd help. I think they're just being nosy and don't like to be left out of anything, but whatever, I'll take the help." She grinned. "I just called them and they'll be over in a few."

"Sounds good. So how are we doing it?"

"I was just planning on doing a horse drive. Since there's only a dozen horses to move over and we aren't going very far, it doesn't make much sense to load them up in the trailer."

"All right, you taking point?"

"Mmm-hmm."

"Okay, I'll get Titus saddled up then."

"I'm glad you aren't using Rex."

He nodded. "Nah, that'd just confuse him. He needs to focus on his training, not doing something new."

She smiled. "Good, that's what I would have suggested. Rex is coming along great but we don't want to do anything to slow down his training."

He winked. "See, I'm not totally clueless."

"You wouldn't be as successful as you are, Brody, if you were even close to clueless. I've seen what you can do."

He stepped toward her. "Oh yeah? You've been following my career?"

She could feel the heat rising across her cheeks.

Brody cupped the back of her neck. He was just bending to kiss her when she heard Duncan. "All right, break it up. I thought we were working here."

Brody pressed a soft, quick kiss on her lips then turned. "We are."

"Just let us saddle up and we'll be ready," Denise told Kasey and Dunc. "Do you want to get all the horses in the corral for me?"

"No problem," Kasey replied. He looked huge on the back of his sorrel. His size should have made him awkward on a horse, yet somehow he was anything but. Kasey was one of the best horsemen around. Not only was he good on a horse, he had this calm, laid-back demeanor, which was soothing to both people and animals. It made him perfect for moving stock.

A few minutes later, they were ready to go. With Brody at her side, she rode up to Kasey and Duncan where they waited patiently by the corral exit. "All right, Dunc, you're on drag. Kase and Brody, you've got flank."

They nodded. "Sounds good."

She eyed the eight cutters she'd been training, and two yearlings who she was acclimatizing to life on a ranch. Those ten, plus Brody's two, made an even dozen to move over to the new stables.

Denise nodded to Brody to let him know she was ready then gave the signal to Duncan to open the gate. The horses quickly fell into line behind her. The three men all knew their place and kept the horses going the way they directed.

About ten minutes later they rode up to the new stables. Denise stopped at the corral and pushed open the gate. The herd of horses all followed her with Duncan closing the gate behind her. "Thanks, guys, we've got it from here," she called out.

"You sure?" Kasey asked.

"Yep, no problem."

Kasey and Duncan tipped their hats then rode off, leaving her and Brody to work.

She wandered around the corral with the horses until their energy leveled off. The little taste of freedom mixed with the confinement in a new surrounding had a few of the horses on edge, which amped up the younger pair.

Denise glanced over at Brody. "I need to get these guys used to their new place, so they know it's safe. Can you put those roping skills to use and grab Sammy so I can introduce him to his new digs?"

"Sure." Brody hopped back up on Titus, opened the gate and slipped in then closed it behind him. He rode up close to Sammy. With just a couple of flicks of his wrist, he had the rope landing securely around the horse's neck.

"Wow, impressive," she told him.

Brody winked. "You ain't seen nothing yet. Wait'll we get a runner then you can be impressed."

She rolled her eyes. "I don't imagine these guys are going to run away since they're pretty trained already."

"I'll wrangle you a calf later then to wow you with my manly charms," he teased.

Denise snorted then mockingly fluttered her hand on her chest. "Oh be still my beating heart, you'd really wrangle a calf for lil'ol' me?"

The corners of Brody's eyes crinkled with amusement. "You betcha, darlin'."

Being with Brody was easy, comfortable. And he certainly knew his way around a ranch. It was nice having him there. She let her gaze linger on the muscles in his forearms, and if watching him made her pulse race a little, well, there was no harm in ogling the eye candy to pass the day. Right?

"I think you've given me a pretty good picture of your manly charms," she told him.

Brody ran his tongue along his bottom lip as he looked at her. She squirmed in her seat. Everything about the man made her hot.

"Oh Dee, we haven't even scratched the surface."

She sucked in a breath. *Oh my. Focus, Dee, now's not the time.* She cleared her throat. "Well, if you play your cards right, cowboy, I just might let you give me another lesson later."

The corner of his lip cocked up slightly as he smirked at her. "Is that right?"

"Mmm-hmm, but you've got to earn it by getting the work done now. No work, no play. And Rex needs his training when we're done here."

He slowly nodded. "All right, boss lady." He pierced her with a heated stare. "But later, you're all mine."

Heat ran through her body. What would he do later? Shoot, she couldn't wait to find out. What had he done to her? It wasn't like her to be willing to chuck work to have sex with a guy. But at this particular moment that's exactly what she wanted to do. Her entire body ached. She wanted him, right here, right now. Lord knows she wanted to say *screw work, let's just go play*. Instead she took a deep breath and exhaled slowly. The practical side of her brain won out.

"Deal. But just so you know, I plan to work you hard today," she told him.

Brody flashed her a sexy-as-sin smile. "That's good, darlin', 'cuz I plan to work you hard tonight."

Her heart pounded so loud she was sure he could hear it. She held her hand to her chest. Tonight couldn't come soon enough.

Chapter Seven

What a difference a week could make. With Justin gone, Denise and Brody fell into a routine. He followed her instructions during the day with what she wanted done on the ranch, how she wanted him to train. And at night she submitted to him and what he wanted. This was exactly what she'd secretly always dreamed of, sharing her life with someone. A man who understood her and her needs and respected her enough to listen when she talked and asked her opinion on how to do things on the ranch. A man who saw her as his equal. Well, except in the bedroom. In there Brody definitely ran the show, which surprisingly was more than fine by her. It was actually freaking amazing if she was honest.

Before Brody, she'd never realized how liberating giving up control in the bedroom could be. How exciting and freeing it would feel with the right guy, someone she trusted to push her limits but not to take it too far.

Brody made her feel safe enough to explore her darkest desires.

After her shower Friday night, Denise rubbed lotion all over her body then fixed her hair and applied a light coating of makeup while Brody grabbed a quick shower. She ran the brush through her hair and debated trying to style it then thought better of it. Brody liked her hair down. He said he liked to have something to hold on to.

Her stomach quivered with anticipation as she wondered what he planned for her tonight. The first couple of nights after her brother left Brody had spent the evening with her then moved over to his trailer to sleep. But for the past week, he'd stopped bothering to put the distance between them and he'd virtually moved in. And she really liked it. Having Brody there, waking up with him in the morning, sharing their meals. It all felt amazing.

During their late-night conversations, they'd talked about their hopes and dreams for the future, what drove them to succeed. With the lights turned low, protected by the darkness at night, Brody had trusted her enough to share things with her about his upbringing that he hadn't told anyone before. How painful it had been growing up the way he had.

With the closeness that had developed between them, she no longer felt like just some girl he was sleeping with. She knew she mattered to Brody more than anyone ever had. He was still slightly guarded but she understood him better and where he was coming from, especially in the bedroom with his need to dominate. With that understanding, she trusted him more and was more willing to go along with what he demanded because she knew ultimately both of their needs would be met.

She didn't want to think about what would happen when Justin came home with Kat and they lost their privacy. Tomorrow she'd check in with the contractor again, maybe she'd be able to move in early. They seemed to be flying along when she popped her head in. It might be worth it to live in a construction zone if it meant she could spend her nights with Brody. She'd sleep on the floor if it meant time alone with him.

The bathroom door opened and Brody walked out with a towel around his hips. Her eyes were drawn to the way his hipbones jutted out, the way his abs formed a V that seemed to point straight down. His cock rose against the towel and she smiled. The man was always ready to go at the drop of a hat.

He walked toward her. "You are gorgeous, Dee."

"Thank you." She looked at him in the mirror. "I wasn't sure if you wanted to go out or stay in so I didn't get dressed yet," she said, fingering the collar of her bathrobe.

Brody rested his hands on her shoulders and smiled. "Definitely in." He pushed her hair off her shoulder and swept it to one side. "I thought it might be fun to do something different tonight."

"Oh yeah? What did you have in mind?"

He trailed his finger lightly down the length of her neck and she shivered beneath his touch. "Have you ever done any sensory play?" he asked.

She wrinkled her brow. What the hell was sensory play? "Umm...not that I know of."

"You'll love it."

Staring at him in the mirror, she didn't blink. Sensory play could be any number of things couldn't it? "What do I have to do?" she asked.

"Just trust me."

"I do," she whispered.

Brody placed a kiss against her nape. "Good."

He moved away from her toward the door.

"Where are you going?" she asked.

"Just grabbing a few things. Lie down on the bed and I'll be right back."

He stepped through the doorway and turned around. "Lose the robe," he ordered as he continued down the hall.

Lose the robe, huh? Nerves jumped in her stomach. What had she just signed on for? She took a deep breath. This was Brody, she trusted him. She exhaled loudly.

When her nerves calmed, she dropped her robe and set it on the edge of the chair then made her way over to the bed. Did he want her on her stomach or back? She chewed her lower lip. Crap, she wished she was more experienced in all this stuff.

Brody came back and she was still standing beside the bed undecided. "I thought I said on the bed."

"You did but I wasn't sure how you wanted me." She looked up at him warily through her lashes. He was carrying a tray filled with food and drinks and a bucket of ice with water bottles and something metal sticking out of it. *Oh boy.*

"Sorry, that's my fault. I should have explained what I wanted. On your back, grab the headboard and spread your legs."

What the hell is the bucket for? Nerves danced in her stomach. Brody raised one eyebrow and stared pointedly at her until she moved.

The cool sheets hit her back as she lay down and she gasped. Brody rested his knee on the edge of the mattress. He eased a cuff around her ankle then looped a rope through it and did the same to the other side, securing her legs to the footboard. He slid up the bed and did the same to her hands. Tied spread-eagle on the bed, she felt incredibly exposed and vulnerable. Anxiety rippled through her with arousal close on its heels. Her nipples beaded tightly beneath his stare.

She didn't know what to expect and not knowing was almost more arousing. He placed a kiss against her lips then produced a scrap of fabric.

"What's that?"

"A blindfold."

"You're going to blindfold me?" She pulled against the straps on her wrists.

"Do you trust me, Dee?"

"Yes," she whispered.

"Good, then relax. You've got your safe word. Use it if you need to but unless I hear it from you I'll assume you're good with anything I'm doing."

She nodded. "Okay."

Brody eased the silk blindfold over her eyes, everything turned black. He rubbed a hand down her arm. "Relax," he murmured.

She inhaled. She could smell strawberries, sort of smelled like her shampoo but stronger. "Why do I smell berries?" she asked.

"Because Shelly went shopping for us."

Secretly, she smiled to herself at the reference to them being a couple. At first he'd been so guarded with everything he'd said and she wasn't sure if he planned on taking a runner or if he expected her to. Now he seemed comfortable with the idea that they weren't temporary, he actually talked somewhat long-term.

Suddenly, something touched her lips and trailed along the seam of her mouth.

"Open," Brody told her.

She opened her mouth and something hard and slightly rough slipped between her teeth.

"Bite."

She bit down and juice burst onto her tongue. Mmm, the strawberries. She moaned.

"Good?"

"Definitely."

With the blindfold on her other senses seemed to be on high alert. She heard the tinkling of something against metal, felt the mattress shift beneath Brody's weight. Every nerve ending shot to life as she strained to figure out what he was doing.

She was concentrating so hard on the sounds she gasped when something soft touched her nipple. A tickle, a caress. What was that? Fabric? A finger? The delicate touch swirled around her breast then tickled its way down her stomach. She arched up to get closer to the teasing touch. It flicked rapidly against her bellybutton. "A feather," she murmured.

"Very good."

Brody's lips wrapped around her nipple and she moaned. The strong suction was a huge contrast to the delicate touch of the feather. Damn, she could really start to like this sensory play thing. Everything Brody did put her body closer to the edge.

The bed shifted then Brody's finger painted her lips with something hot. She opened her mouth and Brody slid his finger inside. "Mmm," she moaned as hot chocolate syrup coated her tongue.

The chocolate mixed with the lingering taste of strawberries. The flavor was exquisite.

She heard the squirt of a bottle a second before something hot hit her nipple in a swirl. She tried to squirm on the bed as the thick, warm liquid oozed down her breast but the ropes held her in place. He'd warmed it to just this side of too hot. It was perfect. Startling, hot, sexy and incredibly erotic. His tongue traced a path along her breast. She could only assume he was licking it off.

Suddenly, he stopped touching her. She waited, wondering what would come next. Nothing. She could hear him breathing, could sense him sitting on the edge of the bed but he didn't touch her. She strained to figure out what was coming next.

Still nothing happened. She was going crazy waiting. Bastard was going to make her beg. She bit her bottom lip hard to make sure she didn't do that.

Brody chuckled. "You doing okay, Dee?"

"Just fine," she said through gritted teeth.

"I can see that."

She growled at the amusement she heard in his voice. He was getting far too much enjoyment out of torturing her. She'd show him. She wouldn't cave, no matter what he did.

Suddenly, hot liquid hit her clit and she screamed. Okay, so much for not caving. Holy crap, that felt amazing. Her pussy throbbed. More hot liquid hit her clit and she bucked her hips. "Brody touch me," she pleaded.

"You want me to touch you?" he asked.

"Yes," she groaned.

"Okay," he said, then placed something ice cold against her hot clit.

"Holy shit," she yelled. The contrast of hot and cold made her pussy feel as if it were going to explode. Her senses were on fire. She didn't know if it was a good thing or bad—all she knew was she wanted to come. Like yesterday.

He alternated a drop of warm liquid against her pussy, then the cold ice. She shivered with arousal. Her nipples were bunched so tightly they hurt. Her pussy throbbed, ached. She just needed to come.

She felt Brody shift his weight so he was lying between her legs, his breath hot on her upper thigh. "God, yes," she moaned. That was what she wanted, his mouth on her. *Please, God, let him do that.*

With her senses on high alert, she could hear her dog whining outside. Just ignore it, she told herself but his whining kept getting louder and louder, distracting her from what Brody was doing to her body. She was so close to orgasm. If only the damn dog would shut up.

Brody ran the ice cube along the right side of her clit, over the hood and down the left side. He placed it inside her pussy. The ice immediately started to melt, the cold liquid slid between her cheeks. She shivered. It was so cold it almost hurt. She moaned and arched.

The dog barked again and she groaned. *Shut up.*

Brody's lips wrapped around her clit. The heat of his mouth burned against her cold clit. She bucked and arched. He inserted his finger into her pussy. Oh god, she was so close. Desperately reaching for her orgasm, she was right on the brink when the dog barked again.

"Ranger," she yelled.

Suddenly, everything stopped. Brody stopped touching her, the blindfold was removed from her face. She blinked rapidly, trying to adjust to the light. What the hell had happened? She'd been so close. Why had he stopped?

Brody stared down at her with a look of concern on his face.

"You okay?" he asked.

"I'd be a lot better if you'd let me finish," she growled. "What kind of sadistic trick was that? You don't get a girl right to the edge like that and then stop."

"You safe-worded, Dee."

"No, I didn't."

"Uh, yeah you did."

"Why would I have done that? I was so close to coming."

He raised his hands, palms up. "I don't know, one minute you were really into it the next you yelled Ranger so I stopped."

She burst out laughing.

"What's so funny?" he asked, his brow furrowed with confusion.

"I wasn't safe-wording. I was yelling at the dog because he was distracting me."

Brody started to laugh. "Shit." He shook his head.

Rancher barked again and they both laughed harder. Tied up, she couldn't contain her laughter the way she normally did so when she tried to breathe she snorted. Loudly. Brody's eyes widened and he laughed harder.

Finally, when they stopped laughing, Brody shook his head. "It seems we picked the wrong safe word."

She giggled. "No kidding. Guess there's a reason you said people use the word red."

He grinned. "Should we switch to red?"

"Probably a good idea," she replied.

He stared down at her then glanced at the tray and sighed. "Looks like the mood on this game has passed."

She wrinkled her nose and nodded. "Sorry."

"No problem." Brody reached up and untied her arms and rubbed them to get the feeling back into place, then did the same with her legs.

"Let me go let Ranger in and I'll be right back." Brody hopped up and grabbed his sweatpants off the top of the laundry basket.

She stared at the way the muscles in his butt flexed as he stepped into them. Mmm, the man had a killer ass.

While she waited for Brody to come back, she adjusted her pillow and pulled the blankets up. She'd just gotten herself all into place and he was back. He kicked off his sweatpants and walked naked back to bed. Still semi-erect it wouldn't take much to get Brody back to being ready for sex.

She shifted on the bed, pretending to get more comfortable so the blanket slipped, exposing her breasts. She saw the heat flare in Brody's eyes.

"Well, I suppose since you ruined my game, you'll have to make it up to me," he told her.

"Oh I will, will I?"

"Absolutely."

Brody propped up the pillow beneath him and tucked an arm behind his head. His cock stood proudly, pushing the blankets off his body. "You're going to have to work hard to make me not regret the interruption."

Payback time. He'd tormented her. It was her turn to give him a little taste of his own medicine. She was going to enjoy seeing him squirm while she pleasured him.

"I'll do my best," she replied. Denise avoided eye contact when she spoke. She was sure he'd see the look in her eye and turn the tables on her if he figured out what she was up to.

She straddled his waist. Brody gripped her ass with his hands and kneaded the muscles. Mmm, that felt good. She shifted. *Focus, Denise, this isn't about your pleasure it's about his and driving him crazy.*

Leaning forward, she sucked his earlobe into her mouth and swirled her tongue. She nibbled her way down his neck. Alternating soft and firm nips, she teased him. His muscles tensed beneath her and he titled his head to the side. She slowly eased her way down his body, swirling her tongue around his nipples. He widened his legs and his cock pulsed against her ass.

She kissed her way down his body and knelt between his legs. His cock was hard and thick, a little bead of moisture coated the tip. Denise licked the drop off and swiped her tongue along the little slit. Brody cleared his throat and she bit back a smile as he shifted. She sucked the head, nibbling it lightly with her lips.

Denise glanced up to find him watching her through hooded eyes. A mocking smile tilted the edge of his lips, a challenge to do her worst.

Okay, so she hadn't hidden her plans very well. She'd show him. Determined to give him the best blowjob of his life, she went back to teasing the head. Watching his face the entire time, she flicked the little piece of skin beneath the head of his cock, then sucked and licked the head.

When Brody looked as if he was starting to really enjoy himself, she changed tactics. She moved down and sucked and licked his testicles, playing with them and licking the little area between his sac and his ass.

"You're playing with fire, Dee," he warned.

She wasn't used to Brody giving her control. She kind of liked it but she knew it wouldn't last. She couldn't wait to find out what he'd do when he took control back. How far he'd push to test her limits and his.

She wanted to push him, drive him to the edge. She ran her tongue along the length of his cock, tracing the vein on the underside of his shaft. She sucked just the head into her mouth.

"I'm done playing." Brody threaded his hands through her hair firmly. "I want to fuck your mouth, so you'd better open up and take it."

Moisture flooded her pussy. Jesus, she loved when he talked like that. She sucked his cock deep.

He fucked her mouth, hitting the back of her throat. Her eyes watered and still she wanted more, needed him to take what he wanted. She relaxed her throat and let Brody fuck her. His fingers dug painfully into her scalp. She could feel the moisture from her pussy running down her legs. God, she was so horny. She loved seeing him like this, hungry and just a little out of control.

He thrust one final time and groaned as his orgasm hit the back of her throat. She swallowed deep, taking every drop.

His grip in her hair eased as his muscles relaxed. "Damn, Dee, that was amazing."

She wiped the edge of her mouth with her finger and smiled, pleased he'd enjoyed it.

Brody shifted and held out his arm for her to lie down with him. "Lie down and go to sleep," he told her.

Huh, he was done? What about her? Puzzled she stared at him, they couldn't be done. He always made sure she had an orgasm and although she was incredibly close already she hadn't finished yet. "But we didn't..."

"I know and we aren't going to."

"But wha...why?"

"You thought it was a good idea to tease me. It's not. So you don't get to come tonight."

"What?" she gasped. He wouldn't really leave her hanging, would he? She looked at him. A glint lit his eyes. Damn it, yes he would just leave her. *Bastard.* She flopped down on the bed.

Brody chuckled. "Don't pout or you won't get off tomorrow either."

Who did he think he was telling her she could or couldn't come? "I'll just take matters into my own hands then," she grumbled.

Brody pushed up onto his elbow and loomed above her. Commanding energy radiated off him, making her pussy weep. Oh she wanted him.

"You'll come when I say you come or you won't come at all. We clear?"

He stared down at her, looking almost angry. Shit, the last thing she wanted to do was piss him off. She looked down. "Yes," she whispered.

"Good," he replied and lay back down.

Denise lay on her side of the bed, praying he wasn't mad at her for pushing him too far.

Brody slid his arm under her head and pulled her toward him. "Stop thinking so hard and go to sleep."

She pushed up so she could see him. "You're not mad at me?"

"No, Dee, I'm not mad at you. We're still learning about each other so you're bound to push my limits. I can't get mad about it but I can get mad if you know the limit and keep pushing. You haven't done that, so we're fine."

She continued to look at him. "Okay so we're good now, but if I choose to take care of things myself we won't be."

He raised an eyebrow. "I guess you've got to decide if you're willing to deal with the punishment for not listening to me."

Memories of the spanking he'd given her flashed through her mind. If that was her punishment, she might be willing to risk it. "What would the punishment be?"

"Not what you're picturing, honey. The punishment should fit the crime."

"What do you mean?"

"You have trouble denying yourself an orgasm so I'll force you to deny it."

"How?"

"You know how on edge you are right now from our playtime?"

She nodded.

"Imagine how much needier you'd feel if I kept doing that to you all night and all through the next day. Getting you so close you almost burst then stopping." A sadistic grin slid across his face. "Think how much you'd need an orgasm then."

That would be sheer torture. She flopped back down on the bed. "I won't touch myself," she grumbled. But only because experience told her he'd reach for her in the middle of the night, wanting her, and she'd get the orgasm she was craving and then some. But if he thought he had to prove a point, he'd prove it and she'd be left hanging. *No thank you.*

If there was one thing she'd learned during their time together it was that controlling things in the bedroom was who Brody was, it was just as much a part of him as breathing. She could try to fight him on it or she could be strong enough to give him what he needed.

Thank goodness she prided herself on being strong because at this moment giving him what he needed kind of sucked. Man, she hoped she was right and he'd make it up to her later. She huffed out a deep breath.

Brody chuckled. "I thought you'd see it my way."

He pulled her toward him and she rested her head against his chest. Even as annoyed as she was by his high-handedness, she craved the connection between them. She'd definitely cruised past being in too deep and ran headfirst into love with the big jerk. And she'd never been happier.

Chapter Eight

The following weekend, Brody rolled over in bed and looked at the clock. Two in the afternoon. He groaned. Justin and his girlfriend would be arriving home any time now. As much as he wanted to spend the day in bed with Denise, he didn't think her brother would appreciate it too much if he came home and found them like this.

He ran his hand down Denise's spine. Her smooth skin tempted him to take her again, but no, he couldn't. He pinched the curve of her ass and she squeaked.

"Ouch."

"Time to get up, darlin'," he murmured.

"No, not yet," she whined and eased back toward him, pressing her ass against his partially erect cock.

"Dee," he groaned.

"Yes," she replied and wiggled her hips. Damn vixen.

He gripped her hip firmly to hold her in place.

"Mmm," she moaned and arched her back, thrusting her breasts up. He laughed to himself. At times he often wondered which one of them was really calling the shots in the bedroom. Sure, he directed things, but her teasing and rubbing definitely got things started on her terms. He wasn't letting her get away with it this time.

He flipped her over onto her back and knelt. He put his legs between hers and widened his stance so she was open to him. He could see how wet she was already.

"You know it's not a good idea to tease me, Dee," he growled.

She wiggled her hips. "No? Why not?" she asked.

"Because payback is a bitch."

She pushed herself up on her elbows. "What do you mean?"

He grabbed the cuffs from the bedside table and wrapped one around each ankle. "Lie down."

The front door slammed shut. It sounded as if Justin and Kat were home.

Denise glanced at the bedroom door. "We should probably get up."

He pushed her feet up so her knees were bent and held her legs there. "Not happening. You had your chance. So lie down."

"Brody," she pleaded. Her nipples pebbled beneath his stare. He trailed a finger through the lips of her pussy and moisture coated his hand. She was drenched. As much as she pretended to protest, the signs of her arousal were clearly visible.

"Lie down," he ordered.

She did as she was told.

"That's better." He grabbed her wrist and wrapped another cuff around it then clipped it to the cuff at her ankle, and did the same on the other side.

"Brody," she pleaded and eyed the door.

He stood and flicked the lock on the door. "Better?"

"I'd be better if you let me go."

"Would you really?" He smirked.

"No," she grumbled.

He lay back down on the bed between her spread knees. The scent of her arousal caressed his senses, teasing him. He spread her with his thumbs. "You're going to pay for teasing me, Dee."

"Brody, no, I don't want anyone to hear me," she whined.

"You should have thought of that, shouldn't you?" he murmured and blew a breath against her wet pussy.

She whimpered. "I'm sorry."

He flattened his tongue and made one long swipe across her slit. Denise groaned.

Moisture coated his tongue. He swirled it around her clit.

"Brody, stop," she moaned even as her hips bucked up to meet him.

"If you really want me to stop, Dee, just say the word," he murmured then swirled his tongue in the other direction, making her groan.

"You're a bastard," she told him.

He laughed. "You love it."

"I know, that's the problem."

He inserted one finger and slowly fucked her with it as he circled his tongue around her tight little bud. Her knees dropped open farther.

Inserting a second finger, he curled them toward the front of her pussy, hitting her G-spot. Denise bucked and moaned loudly.

He glanced up. Denise bit her bottom lip between her teeth as she whimpered beneath his touch.

Fucking her with his finger, he increased the tempo. He sucked her clit into his mouth. Denise's breath came hard and fast, panting. Her pussy clenched against his fingers.

"Oh god, Brody."

He took her clit between his teeth and bit, sending her skyrocketing toward orgasm. Her pussy milked his fingers. Man, he wished he could fuck her and suck her at the same time so he could feel her in his mouth and on his cock when she came like this.

He continued to suck on her clit then slowly swirled his tongue around the tight bud, bringing her down until the muscles of her pussy stopped constricting around his finger.

Denise's eyes fluttered open. "Wow."

He placed a kiss against her pussy then pushed himself up.

Kneeling between her legs, he reached over and grabbed a condom from the bedside table. He tore the wrapper open with his teeth and sheathed himself.

Looking over at Denise with her hands and ankles cuffed, spread wide for him, his dick throbbed. God, she looked beautiful. He couldn't wait to bury himself inside her.

He positioned himself between her legs and placed his cock at her entrance. He held her stare and she smiled. His breath caught at the look on her face. So trusting and open. He wasn't sure he deserved this kind of caring but everything in him wanted to earn it.

Brody pressed in a little at a time, going slow. Denise's eyes drifted shut and her back arched.

He eased back then forward. He wanted to make it last. To drag out this last time together before the real world with her family and friends intruded.

Reaching between them, he flicked his finger against her clit.

"Yes," Denise hissed.

He continued to swirl around her clit as he thrust. Her pussy started to flex around his cock. Her breathing got louder. "God, Brody, yes," she moaned.

He pinched her clit between his fingers and she screamed out her orgasm. His balls drew up tight. Her pussy gripped his cock like a glove, dragging him quickly toward his own release. She opened her eyes and smiled. He'd wanted to make it last but feeling her come around him and seeing the look in her eyes was more than he could take. He thrust once, twice more and groaned as he came.

Brody kissed her lips, his tongue tangled with hers. He felt her shift beneath him. Damn her cuffs. As much as he wanted to just enjoy this moment, he couldn't leave her like that.

He unbuckled the clips and pulled the cuff from one ankle then the other. Denise stretched her legs out on the bed and sighed. "Mmm, that feels good."

Brody laughed. "You aren't supposed to make sex sounds when I release you, you know."

Denise giggled. "Sorry."

He undid the cuffs at her wrists and tossed them into the bedside table. The last thing they needed was her brother seeing those.

When they walked into the kitchen several minutes later, an attractive blonde pushed away from the counter and wrapped her arms around Denise. The woman was several inches shorter than Dee but it didn't slow her down any. Denise laughed and hugged the woman back. This must be the soon-to-be sister-in-law Kat. Having been friends with Justin for years, he did what any good buddy would do. He checked out his friend's girl. The woman was attractive and he could definitely see what caught Justin's eye but next to Denise the busty blonde couldn't even come close. He ignored the little warning in the pit of his stomach that said there was something wrong when a gorgeous woman didn't even make a blip on his radar.

The two women separated and the little blonde gave Brody the once-over.

"You must be Brody. I've heard a lot about you," Kat said with a smirk.

"I am, yeah. You must be Kat. It's nice to meet you too," Brody said and stuck out his hand to shake hers.

Kat leaned back against the island. "So, Dee, did you enjoy having the house all to yourself?"

Justin scowled, making Kat laugh. "What? It's a legitimate question."

Brody liked the other woman already.

"Yeah, it was nice," Dee replied and looked over at Brody. The look she gave him told him how much she'd enjoycd their time together.

"Did you practice running around naked?" Kat asked.

"Kat, gross, that's my sister," Justin grumbled.

"What? I told her that was one of the best things about living alone. You didn't have to get dressed if you didn't want to."

Justin stared at his fiancée and Brody could feel the heat between them from across the room.

Brody eyed Denise and she wrinkled her nose. They needed to change the subject. "So, Kat, Justin said you were writing an article? What was it about?"

Thank you, Denise mouthed. He nodded.

Just as Kat started to reply the back door slammed.

"Hey, hey, the great travelers have returned," Kasey called out as he walked into the kitchen with a package tucked under his arm. Duncan followed behind with a case of beer under his.

"Kitty Kat, get over here," Duncan called.

Kat squealed and ran across the room. She threw her arms around Duncan and placed a smacking kiss on his lips then turned to Kasey and did the same thing.

There was nothing sexual about the kiss but still Brody looked over at Justin. He couldn't believe the other man wasn't ready to pound on his friends for even daring to lay a hand on his woman. But Justin looked fine. In fact, he just rolled his eyes and laughed. "Keep your hands off her ass, Dunc."

"Ah come on, you know she likes it," Duncan teased. "Besides, after being cooped up with you for the past two weeks she's probably dying for a change of menu. Why don't you run away with Kase and me, Kat?"

Kat cocked her head to the side as if she was seriously considering the offer then shook her head. "Nah, I've almost got Justin broken in. I've invested too much training in him to start all over. Sorry, guys."

Justin growled then wrapped his arms around Kat from behind and nipped her neck. "Keep it up, woman."

Kat giggled.

Denise smacked her brother on the arm as she walked past. "Didn't you two get enough of each other the past two weeks?"

"Nope," Justin murmured as he nuzzled Kat's neck.

Brody watched the interplay between everyone. They were such a close unit. A real family, despite the fact only Justin and Dee were related by blood. He'd never had that with anyone. Even with his roping partner Cord, they were friends but he didn't have the same kind of connection with him this group seemed to have with each other.

Denise came up beside him and snuggled against him. "You okay?" she asked.

"Sure, of course."

"What are you thinking about?"

"Nothing much. Just watching. Kat seems great."

Denise smiled. "Yeah, she is. She makes my brother happy so that's all I care about."

"Yeah, but she fits too."

"What do you mean?"

He shrugged. "I don't know. She just seems like she fits your group."

Denise seemed to think about what he said then nodded. "You're right, she does. But then so do you."

"Me?"

"Mmm-hmm. The guys like you, that doesn't happen with men I date."

"They knew me before."

"No, that's not it. I've dated other guys they knew and it was different, awkward. With you it doesn't feel uncomfortable."

No, not anymore, but when he'd first arrived the guys hadn't made it overly comfortable for him. Now that Denise and he were together they seemed to have accepted it in stride but he was under no illusions about where their loyalty lay. They were his friends but Denise was their family. And family was everything. He absently rubbed his hand against the ache in his chest. Not that he'd ever admit it to anyone but he longed to be part of a family. Watching them together made him realize how much he wanted this for himself. But he didn't have a clue how to have it. As much as Denise thought he fit in her group, he knew he was only here because of her and without Dee he'd be tossed out on his ear. Things between them were great now, but sooner or later she'd wise up and realize she wanted more than a guy like him could offer. It's not as if he could expect a woman like Denise to wait around forever for him to get his shit together.

He kissed Denise on the top of the head. "Thanks for including me."

She turned and looked up at him and smiled. "My pleasure."

Brody wrapped his arms around her waist and pulled her against him. Denise wasn't like the women he normally dated, but she got to him in a way no one else ever had. She made him want. Not just her, but a life that had more to it than traveling from place to place and woman to woman. He took a deep breath and exhaled. Unfortunately, he didn't know the first thing about making a normal relationship work. His role models growing up were the epitome of dysfunction. And the few times he'd tried to have a relationship himself over the years it had shown him he hadn't learned from the best. If he was smart, he'd just enjoy this while it lasted rather than getting caught up imagining what could be.

A woman like Denise would never be with a guy like him long-term. She was all about family, heritage and history and he didn't have any of that. His family history was definitely nothing to be proud of. Lord knows he'd like nothing more than to change all that. He dreamed about getting a place of his own and having enough money in the bank that no one could ever take it away from him. Then maybe he'd be on the road to being worthy of her. But even then, he still didn't know the first thing about being a stable guy. He'd spent his life wandering from place to place. He didn't even know if he had it in him to stay in one place long-term.

"Brod, let's go," Kasey called.

Dragging his attention away from Denise, he glanced over at the three men standing at the doorway. "Go where?"

"It's guy time. Ruff ruff ruff," they grunted like Tim-the-Tool-Man Taylor.

"Guy time?"

"Yeah, we're manning the grill. Let the ladies do their girly thing in here with vegetables and crap," Duncan said.

Brody glanced down at Denise as she glared at the trio of men. He bit back a laugh. They'd be lucky to make it out with their balls intact if they talked too much like that around her.

"Duncan, honey, you want to be able to use that tool you think makes you a man?" Denise asked.

Duncan grinned. "Yeah."

"Then cut the bullshit."

Brody snorted. Denise gave him the evil eye. "That goes for you too, buddy."

"What did I do?" Brody asked.

"You're a guy and you're the closest one to me."

"Well in that case, I think I'll go help the guys with the barbecue."

"Coward," she muttered.

He laughed. "I call it smart enough to get reinforcements."

"Fine, but you better cook my meat properly."

He nipped her earlobe. "Darlin', don't you worry, I know exactly how you like your meat."

Denise rolled her eyes. "Oh my god, just go," she said and shoved him on the arm.

Laughing, he followed the guys outside.

Outside on the patio, Brody followed Duncan over to the table while Justin and Kasey headed over to the huge built-in grill. The whole thing looked like something out of a design magazine.

"Nice setup," Brody muttered.

Justin grinned. "I know, it's awesome." He flicked a switch on the wall and music poured through the outdoor speakers.

Kasey put the case of beer in the outdoor fridge and pulled out four cold ones. He handed one to Justin, then sat down at the table and pushed two beers across for Brody and Duncan.

Brody had just taken the first swig of icy cold beer when Justin asked, "So what are your intentions with my sister?"

Choking back the mouthful of liquid, he looked up to find three sets of eyes focused on him.

"W-wha..." Brody stammered.

"Your intentions? How do you see this thing between you two playing out?" Justin demanded.

"Well, we haven't really talked about it much." What was with these guys? From everything he knew about Denise, she could take care of herself. Hell, she was more independent than most people he knew, male or female. There didn't seem to be anything she was afraid to tackle.

"Don't you think you should?" Kasey asked.

"Yeah, I guess, but I kind of thought that was between Dee and me, not you guys."

Justin tilted his beer bottle on the table. A bead of moisture ran down the brown glass. "She's my sister, man. She's not going to deal well with you two going your separate ways."

"What are you talking about? Why would we go our separate ways?"

"Aren't you?" Justin stared at him with this knowing look on his face that Brody wanted to smack off.

He glanced across the patio and into the kitchen window. Denise stood at the counter with her head thrown back, laughing at something Kat was saying. His heart hammered in his chest. There was no way he was walking away from her. He might not be the kind of guy she ultimately wanted to end up with. But he wasn't stupid enough to bail out before she figured that out.

As if she could sense him watching her, Denise turned and looked out the window. When their eyes met, a slow smile spread across her full lips. Shit, he was done.

"No, we're definitely not going our separate ways," he muttered to no one in particular.

"How do you see that playing out with you on the road?" Duncan asked.

Unable to take his eyes off Denise, he replied, "I don't know, man, but we'll figure something out." He didn't have a clue how they'd make it work. The whole idea was somewhat overwhelming, just the logistics of everything.

He tore his stare away from her and took a sip of beer. Deep down there was a niggling whisper inside him that said Denise would never stay with him, no one ever did. Trying to ignore the voice in his head, he downed the rest of his beer. He'd cross that bridge when he had to.

Chapter Nine

Two weeks later, the morning sun streamed through the window as they lay in bed. As amazing as snuggling with Brody was, she couldn't spend all day here. She mentally started running over her mile-long to-do list. She'd talked to the contractor yesterday and it looked as if her house would be ready to move into next week. So much for their three- to four-week estimate, they were now sitting at six and still had a week to go. Even with the extra time, she still wasn't ready. Somehow she'd been so wrapped up with Brody she hadn't managed to do several of the things on her list. Furniture was her top priority.

She ran her hand down Brody's naked chest, tracing the ridges of muscles as she moved.

How was it possible Brody had been here almost two months already? In some ways it seemed as if he'd just arrived and in others it seemed as if he'd always been there he fit so well. She couldn't imagine her life without him now.

Denise rolled over and pushed herself up on Brody's chest so she could look at his face. "I was thinking it might be fun to go shopping this weekend for some new bedroom furniture for the house. Get a king-sized bed, maybe something with a good headboard." She winked.

He grimaced. Typical man, mention the word shopping and he looked as if you'd just suggested Chinese water torture. "Come on, it'll be fun. This way you get some say in things."

"Why do I need a say in things?"

"I just assumed you'd be coming back here on your weekends off."

"Yeah, I was planning on it."

"Right, so it makes sense for you to help pick stuff that you like too."

"It's not really my place, Dee, it's yours."

"I know technically it is but…"

"But what?"

Studying the wary look on his face, she tried to formulate a way to ask him to stay.

"I can almost hear the wheels turning in there, Dee. What's up?"

"Umm…you know how we were talking about how you'd like to have a home base at some point to go to between competitions?" she asked.

"Mmm-hmm."

"Well I was thinking maybe this could be your home?"

"What do you mean this? Like here, your place?"

She winced at the incredulous tone of his voice. "Yeah."

Brody snorted. "No."

Pain lanced through her. "Why not? What's wrong with my place?"

"Nothing, it's great, it's just…" He shrugged. "It's just not mine."

"But it could be…I mean if you wanted it to be."

"Dee, no it couldn't. This place belongs to you and your brother. I can't mooch off you." He shook his head. "No, I'm not that guy."

"Who said anything about mooching? You've worked on the ranch the entire time you've been here. And you'd help out when you came back. I don't see the problem."

"No, you wouldn't because it's your place."

"What's that supposed to mean?"

"Nothing, it's just different when you're the owner than it is when you're a hired hand. That's just not me. I always dreamed of more for myself then working for my girlfriend."

Every muscle in her body went rigid. "But nothing personal right?" she asked sarcastically.

He sat up and leaned against the headboard. He scrubbed a hand over his face. "It's got nothing to do with you, Dee."

"Right." She sat up cross-legged on the bed and faced him. Tugging the sheet up, she wrapped the fabric under her arms so her chest was covered. He'd seen her naked enough times it shouldn't matter but this time was different. She needed the security the thin sheet provided.

"Dee, don't be like that," he grumbled.

"No, sorry. This is how I'm going to be. So you can't have this as your home base, not because you don't care about me enough to be with me but because it's my place, not yours."

"Yeah, basically."

"So where did you see this going exactly, Brody?"

"I don't know. I figured I'd keep my eyes open for a place and when I found something, I was hoping you'd move there with me."

Dumbfounded, she stared at him. "Are you fucking kidding me?"

"What? I thought you said you wanted to be together."

"Yeah, I did." She exhaled audibly. He couldn't be serious. "Let me get this straight. It's fine for me to give up everything I've built, my life, to move in with you but it's not okay for you to move in with me?"

"It's different."

"You're right, it's completely different. I already have a place, a business I've worked damn hard to establish, something I'm proud of. While you're basically homeless and somehow I should just give that all up because you don't feel like a man if you're not the owner."

"It's not like that," he growled.

"No? Then how is it, big guy? Explain to me how what you want is more important than what I want."

"It's not. Come on, Denise, you're being ridiculous. You could set up a training facility anywhere and be successful."

"But why should I? I already have that. I've busted my ass for years creating what I have and you want me to just chuck that away for nothing."

"It's not for nothing, it's for us."

"How's it for us? Explain that to me." How could giving up her life be best for them? That didn't even make sense.

"Dee, try to look at it from my point of view, would you? What kind of man would I be if I let you take care of me?"

She laughed but the sound held no humor. "What kind of woman would I be if I let you take care of me?"

"It's not the same and you know it," he snapped.

Tears welled up behind her eyes and she fought to keep them at bay. She couldn't cry. That was exactly what he expected her to do. After all, women were emotional and weak. Well not her. She'd known getting involved with Brody was a bad idea but he'd said all the right words and made her think he was different. He wasn't. He was the same as every other guy.

She stood, taking the sheet with her. She couldn't be around him anymore.

"Dee, where are you going?"

"We're done. Pack up your shit and go. Don't bother coming back."

Brody vaulted off the bed and stood in front of her completely naked, anger radiated off him in waves. "You're breaking up with me over a fight?"

"No, Brody, I'm breaking up with you because you're full of shit."

His jaw clenched. "How so?"

"Oh, you're good, I'll give you that. You had me convinced you actually believed all that bullshit you spewed about us being equals."

"It wasn't bullshit. We are equals."

"Clearly." The sarcasm rolled off her tongue with a steel edge. God, she was an idiot. She'd gone and fallen in love with a guy who was exactly the kind of man she'd always sworn to avoid.

"When have I ever treated you like we aren't equals? Hell, you run the show when we're training because it's your area of expertise."

"No, Brody, we're equals when it's convenient but deep down you don't see me that way. If you did moving here wouldn't be a big deal. It'd be no different than the woman moving in with the man if the situation was reversed. But the situation isn't reversed, Brody. You're asking me to give up everything, not just the business that I've created but the life that I've created. My home, my family." She shook her head. "I thought you were so much more than that. What we had was so much more."

"It's not the same thing, Dee."

"No, you're right, it's not. It would be one thing to give that up if you had the same thing somewhere but you don't. You've got shit. I'm offering you the chance to finally have a home, not a house, Brody, a home. A place where you belong and you're too chauvinistic to accept that because it makes you feel like less of a man to move in with a woman." She angrily wiped the tears that were streaming down her face. So much for not being the emotional girl.

"Dee."

She held up her hand. "Just go, Brody."

"Dee, let's talk about this."

She smiled sadly. "I wish there was something to talk about, but there's not." With that, she scooped her clothes off the floor and walked out of the room, leaving what she had thought was her future behind her.

Brody stood in the bedroom after Denise left and stared after her. His mind replayed everything they'd talked about. How had they gone from discussing moving in together permanently to breaking up? It had happened in a heartbeat. She hadn't even given him a second to process before she attacked. Had he come across like a jerk? Maybe. But the woman went from zero to a hundred in the blink of an eye. One second she was hearts and roses and the next she had her gun cocked and ready with no time to breathe in between.

If he mattered to her as much as she claimed, didn't he at least deserve a chance to explain how she'd blindsided him? How he'd needed a second to formulate some kind of response. Hell, a chance to explain what he'd meant before she dumped his ass. She hadn't cared about him enough to give him the benefit of the doubt at all. Just like everyone else he'd ever known.

He shoved his legs into his jeans. Scanning the room, he spotted his t-shirt hanging off the edge of the dresser where it had landed in the heat of things the night before. He grabbed the shirt and started to pull it on but his head got stuck in the neck hole. Pissed off, he yanked harder. The fabric ripped beneath the pressure, which pissed him off more. Just great.

Dressed, Brody stormed out of the room and down the hall. Instead of stopping in the kitchen like he normally did each morning he kept right on going out the door. He didn't stop moving until he had the horses loaded up in the trailer and he was on the road. He probably should have tried to find Denise but he'd been too angry to talk rationally.

Unfortunately, the drive to Texas gave him way too much time to think. Instead of talking himself down he just got more and more angry. Maybe she was right and they were better off going their separate ways. They were too different. Denise was a home-and-hearth kind of person. She was all about family. It was everything to her and he didn't know the first thing about being a part of something like that. Hell, he didn't even know where he belonged.

Rodeo was the only thing that had ever made sense to him. He could still remember his first one. He'd been struggling to get a grip on things in his fifth foster home in two years and been acting out. His foster parents had made him go with them to the rodeo. It was supposed to have been a punishment, forcing him to spend the day with them rather than going out with his friends. But when he'd seen the horses and felt the energy, he'd felt connected to something for the first time in his life.

Those foster parents hadn't lasted—like all the others before and after—but the connection to the rodeo had. And when he'd turned eighteen, he'd taken every penny he could scrounge, hit the circuit and never looked back.

He'd felt the connection, that bone-deep yearning, with Denise too, but this time instead of being exciting it terrified him. He didn't know the first thing about making a relationship work long-term. He didn't know the first thing about having a home. Maybe it was better this way. She'd find a better guy who fit into her life and he'd keep doing what he was doing for as long as he could, then eventually he'd find a place to lay his hat on a more permanent basis.

It seemed like a great idea until he pulled his trailer into the campground and glanced at the site beside him where his roping partner and his family had set up and a wave of longing tore through him like he'd never felt before. *Damn it.*

The past couple of weeks without Brody had been torture. She'd cried more in the past two weeks than she had in her entire life. What was she going to do? How was she supposed to get over Brody when everything reminded her of him?

Denise paced around the kitchen. She spun around and nearly bumped into Kat.

"Sorry," Denise mumbled.

Kat handed her a knife and a bag of peppers. "Here. Make yourself useful. You can take out all that energy on the cutting board."

Slapping the cutting board down onto the counter, Denise sighed. She was a wreck. "Do you think I should go see him?"

"Why? You broke up."

"I know, we did, but..." She paused and slid her knife through the center of the red pepper and ripped out the core. "He's not doing well. If he doesn't start winning some purses, he's not going to get the buckle this year."

Kat leaned her hip against the counter. "So?"

Denise rolled her eyes. "I trained the horse. If he's not ready then I feel bad."

"Is that all?" Kat asked.

"Of course." Dee slammed her knife through the flesh of the pepper.

"Yeah, I can tell you've got nothing else on your mind other than making sure you trained the best horse you could," Kat said.

Denise raised her head and snarled at her soon-to-be sister-in-law. "Shut up."

Kat laughed. "If you want to go to him because you want to see him then do it, you don't need to make excuses with me."

"I'm not making excuses," she grumbled.

"Dee, come on, this is me you're talking to."

"Fine, I want to see him, but it's stupid. What's the point? It's not like we can ever be together."

"No, not if neither of you are willing to make a compromise."

"It's not a compromise, Kat. It's giving up who I am for a guy."

Kat shrugged. "That's one way to look at it, but then I'm probably the wrong person to talk to about this. After all, I moved across the country to be with your brother."

"That's not the same thing."

Kat raised her eyebrow. "How's it not?"

"It just made sense for you to move here, Justin's life is here."

"So? My life was in New York." Kat put her hand on her hip and stared at Denise.

"Yeah, but Justin and I have the ranch, it's not like either of us could pick up and leave so it makes sense for you and Brody to move here."

"Sure, on some level. But that wasn't the only deciding factor."

"What do you mean? What else is there?"

"I don't know, Dee." Kat sighed. "It just wasn't as easy a decision for me to move as you think it was. I gave up a lot to be with your brother. My family is back east, my friends, my job. My life. I had some baggage to deal with before I was fully ready to move and from everything you've told me about Brody I'm sure he has lots of baggage of his own."

"I get what you're saying, Kat, I do. But it's still not the same thing. Brody doesn't have any of that. He doesn't have a home, a family, he never has, so I'm not asking him to give it up."

"No, but did you ever think maybe because he's never had a home it's more important to him to create that for himself, to build that on his own rather than to come into something that's already established?"

The revelation hit her like a kick to the head. She slumped against the counter. Was Kat right? Was that what Brody had really meant?

"Something to think about." Kat squeezed Denise's shoulder then walked out of the kitchen, leaving her alone.

As she sat in the kitchen, she dimly registered the sound of a big diesel truck engine near the house.

She replayed her last conversation with Brody. No, she couldn't have misunderstood what he'd been saying.

The sound of men arguing pulled her from her contemplation. A girl couldn't even hear herself think in this place.

She threw open the kitchen door and stormed outside. Following the voices, she headed toward the front. When she rounded the house, she stopped dead in her tracks. Brody. Her breath was sucked out of her at the sight of him going toe-to-toe, arguing with Kasey. What was he doing here?

Kasey pushed Brody in the chest. "I told you if you hurt her I'd kick your ass."

"Give it your best shot, tough guy, because I'm not leaving without talking to her."

Kasey shoved Brody again. Brody shoved back.

Oh god, the last thing she wanted was either of them to get hurt. Denise ran across the yard. "Enough, you two, stop it." At the sound of her voice, Brody's head turned toward her just as Kasey threw the first punch. It landed square on Brody's jaw and he staggered.

"Kasey, no," she yelled.

Kasey turned just as she ran up to him. She held his arm. "Enough. I appreciate the thought but it's not your fight."

"Damn it, Dee, he made you cry. Beating the shit out of him is the least he deserves."

"Kase, it's okay. Honest." She cupped her friend's cheek. "I got this, trust me."

Kasey stared at her then nodded.

She turned to face Brody. He stood, rubbing his jaw, watching her warily. The past two weeks hadn't been easy on him either. His eyes were shadowed, his hair scraggly. It didn't look as if he'd shaved since he left.

"What are you doing here, Brody?"

"Can we talk?"

"Go for it."

He stood up straight and walked toward her. Kasey growled in warning and she turned and scowled at him.

"Fine," Kasey muttered.

Brody stared at her, his eyes roaming across her body. She wondered if he was cataloging how hard the passage of time had been on her the same way she'd noticed the wear and tear on him.

"Can we maybe talk in private?" he asked as he eyed Kasey over her shoulder.

"Fine."

Chapter Ten

She led the way to his trailer. At least if they talked in his place, she wouldn't have a constant reminder of the conversation if things went wrong. For the past two weeks, every time she walked into her bedroom she cringed as memories of their time together and their last conversation all swirled together into one giant emotional vortex she couldn't seem to get out of.

Inside the trailer, Denise sat down on the couch and clasped her hands in her lap. What was Brody doing here? Did he want her back? Oh god, what if he was just here because of Rex? She took a deep breath. Whatever it was she'd handle it. She had to.

"Do you want a drink or anything?" Brody asked. He tossed his cowboy hat onto the counter while he waited for her to reply.

Her throat felt like sandpaper. She didn't think she'd be able to swallow her own spit, let alone a drink right now. "No thanks." Her voice sounded gravelly, even to her ears.

"You sure?"

She nodded.

Brody sat on the opposite end of the couch and rested his arms on his knees. He turned his head to look at her. "You've messed me up, Dee."

"I've messed you up?"

"You obviously haven't been following my stats. I mean, why would you? But they're pretty fucking awful."

"Is Rex not performing?" *God, please don't make him be here about the horse. Please, please, please.*

"I wish Rex was the problem." He ran a hand through his sandy-blond hair. "What the hell did you do to me, Dee? I can't get my head in the game."

"And that's my fault?"

"Yeah. I can't sleep, I can't think. The horses are picking up on my mood and they're doing their own thing." He shook his head. "I don't know what to do. That part of my life has always made sense to me. No matter what else was going on with me, when I got on a horse with a rope in my hand, everything else just faded away. But now?" He sighed. "Now you're there constantly and I can't compartmentalize it like I normally can. You're in my head when I ride, whispering about the horses cues and what to watch for."

Sadness swamped her. If only that was enough. "I don't know what you want me to say, Brody."

"I want you to say you made a mistake ending it. I want you to say you're as miserable as I am."

"I am, but I don't know how to change things between us. As much as I love you, I'm not willing to throw everything I've worked for away."

"You love me?" he asked.

She rolled her eyes. "Of course I love you. I wouldn't have been talking about you moving in with me if I didn't love you."

A slow, sexy smile slid across his face. "Good. I'm glad."

She huffed, completely exasperated by him. How could he say it was good? They were still in the same predicament. "How's it good?"

"Because maybe we can figure all the other shit out if we've got that."

"We don't have that either, you don't love me." If he did, he'd never have asked her to give up her home.

"Don't I?"

Hope sprang in her chest. "Do you?" she whispered. Was it possible that he really did love her?

"God, Dee, that's what I've been trying to say. You make me completely crazy but yeah, I love you."

"But you still don't understand me, Brody."

His forehead wrinkled with confusion. "How do I not understand you?"

"I thought you did, you seemed to. We'd agreed to keep the dominance thing in the bedroom, but everywhere else we'd be equals. But when push came to shove that's not what you wanted," she told him.

Brody pinched the bridge of his nose and exhaled audibly. "That wasn't it at all. It was just the whole conversation surprised me and I guess I didn't handle it very well."

"Okay, so where does that leave us?" She watched him, hoping he'd say the right thing, that he really did see her as his equal.

He exhaled audibly. "Do we have to decide today?"

She sighed. "I think we do. I'm not going to change my mind, Brod. I can't give this all up, even for you. I'd resent you too much and that wouldn't work."

"I kind of figured you'd say that."

"So we're back to where we started." A tear rolled down her cheek. "Maybe loving each other isn't enough."

"It's more than enough."

"How can you say that? You still need to be the man and support the little woman."

His head snapped back and his eyes widened. "What?"

"Isn't that why you wouldn't move here with me?"

"No, being a man had nothing to do with it. I'm pretty sure there's no doubt on that one." He stood and paced around the small living room. "It's not about money and needing to be the breadwinner for us, Dee."

"Then what's it about?"

He rubbed the back of his neck. "I don't know. I'm not the kind of guy who can take a handout. I guess I need to know I helped build it, that I'm not just coasting on someone else's hard work."

That's exactly what Kat had said. "Okay, so if we could figure out a way for you to feel like you have a hand in creating a life here you'd be fine with everything?"

He shrugged. "I don't know, maybe."

"Maybe? I don't get it, Brody. If it's not about you being the man then I don't understand why you can't build something here that you feel is yours."

He paced toward the back of the trailer. "I'm just not sure it's possible, everything here is so established."

"True, but there's always room for improvement and growth. Look at how much I've changed things recently," she replied. Her mind scrambled for something to grasp on to. A way to make it work. There had to be a solution.

He stopped in front of her and knelt down so they were eye level. "Look, Dee, I don't know what the answer is but I know I'm not willing to let you go." He sighed. "I was an idiot. What you have already is exactly what I've always wanted and I can't ask you to give that up."

She cupped his cheeks between her hands. "Thank you for understanding." She kissed his lips. "We'll figure something out."

He nodded.

"I missed you," she whispered.

"Good." He stood and pulled her to her feet. "Show me."

Her insides quivered at the commanding tone in his voice. God, she'd missed that. She couldn't imagine giving up control in the bedroom to anyone but Brody. She trusted him in a way she couldn't trust anyone else. Even though he was in control, she felt as if they were on the same playing field. He needed this as much as she did.

She lowered her eyes. "What would you like me to do?"

A shudder ran through his powerful body. He was as affected by her as she was by him. Maybe even in this they were more equal than she'd ever realized.

"Come here," he said and held out his hand.

Like a lamb to the slaughter, she went to him, willing to do whatever he wanted. He was right. No matter what, they could figure it out and make it work. Love was a gift and she couldn't just toss it away.

She took Brody's hand. He cupped the back of her neck and pulled her toward him. He inhaled deeply. "Jesus, I even missed the way you smell."

"I know what you mean," she said and cuddled against him. She'd missed so many little things about him as well.

His big, strong arms wrapped around her. She'd missed him so much, even just the way she fit perfectly against him. The way his hips pressed against hers, how her head rested just right against his shoulder even when they were standing.

Brody kissed her lips, softly at first but the kiss quickly escalated. Hungry, they both fought for more, their tongues tangled. He cupped her ass with both of his hands and picked her up. She wrapped her legs around his waist. There weren't many guys big enough to pick up her almost six-foot frame, but even in this they were perfectly matched. As he carried her to the bed, she didn't feel as if he was going to drop her. She felt safe and protected.

Brody stopped at the edge of the bed and set her down. He slowly undid the buttons of her shirt and eased the fabric off her shoulders. His calloused hands caressed her arms, sending a shiver down her spine. He unhooked her bra and tossed it to the side. He cupped her breasts and pressed them together. Bending slightly, he swirled his tongue around one nipple then the other. She dropped her head back and closed her eyes.

He drew her right nipple in firmly and pressed it against the roof of his mouth. Denise sucked in a breath. He continued to play with her nipples while he undid her pants and she kicked them off, her panties quickly followed suit.

Brody stepped back and looked at her. "You are so beautiful, Dee."

His eyes were dark with lust, his nostrils flared as he stared at her. She cocked her head to the side and smiled. "Better than those bunnies who are always hitting on you?"

"It's not even a contest," he said reverently.

"I'm glad you like the way I look," she told him.

"Honey, I more than like it."

"Can I help you get undressed?" she asked.

Brody groaned. "Absolutely."

Denise gripped the edge of his shirt, pulled it over his head and tossed it on the chair by her bra. She knelt down so she was eye level with his crotch. His hard cock strained against his jeans. Needing to touch him, she rubbed her hand over it.

Moisture coated the inside of her thighs as she shifted closer to him on her knees. She undid his pants and pulled them down with his underwear in one sweep. His cock stood out proudly from his muscular body, calling her. Her mouth watered. Denise looked up and met Brody's heated stare. "Dee," he said.

"Please," she pleaded. She wanted to pleasure him.

He nodded and threaded his hands through her hair.

She ran her tongue over the head of his cock and moaned. His pre-cum dripped across her tongue. Mmm, he tasted good.

Licking and sucking, she played with his cock until Brody grabbed a fistful of hair and pulled her back. "As great as your mouth is, when I come I want to be balls-deep in your hot pussy."

"Mmm, sounds good to me."

Brody took her arm and pulled her upright. He picked her up and set her on the bed then crawled up beside her. He sat down in the middle of the mattress with his legs out. "Come here," he told her.

Denise wrinkled her brow. What exactly did he have planned? She crawled across the mattress and knelt beside him.

Brody grabbed her hips and picked her up so she sat straddling his lap. His hard cock pressed up between them. He threaded his hand through her hair and guided her mouth to his for a hot, searing kiss that made her toes curl.

He didn't ease up on the kiss. His tongue tangled with hers until she was squirming against him so hot she was sure she'd come as soon as he touched her.

Brody leaned back and grabbed a condom. He slid it on then looked at her, searing her with a hungry look. "Put me inside you," he ordered.

She arched her hips, placed his cock at her entrance and slid down. She was so wet she barely needed to even move to accommodate his large size.

"Mmm," she moaned.

When he was fully seated inside her, Brody pressed against the middle of her chest. "Lie back."

She lay down and he placed a pillow under her hips. He moved a little and she gasped. "Oh my."

A slow smile spread across his face. "Guess I hit my spot." He rocked forward and she groaned. "Yep, I'm definitely in the right place."

Somehow that little movement was more intense than the hardest pounding. Not that she didn't love both methods, but she'd never expected such a little stroke to feel so incredible.

He moved again ever so slightly. She arched her back and her eyes drifted shut.

"Eyes on me, Dee," he said.

She looked up at him. With his beard and scraggly hair he should have looked unkempt. Instead, he looked incredibly sexy. She could see the love in his eyes as he held her with his heated stare.

He reached between them and rubbed her clit with his finger. Between his cock hitting her G-spot and his magical hands she was on the verge of orgasm within seconds. The muscles in her pussy clenched tightly, trying to hold him in place as he moved in and out.

She wrapped her fists into the blanket and fought to keep her eyes on Brody. She wanted to wait for him so they could orgasm together. He pinched her clit and she bit her lip to fight back the explosion that threatened to overtake her. He grinned. "Go ahead, honey, come."

He pinched her clit again and she bowed off the bed as an orgasm tore through her.

She sagged against him and gasped for breath.

When she opened her eyes, Brody smiled down at her. "Did you finish?" she asked.

"Not yet." He pushed his feet under him so he was kneeling between her legs.

The aftershocks of her orgasm made her pussy contract around him and Brody groaned.

He pushed her knees up to her chest. "Hold your legs there," he ordered.

The new position made him feel so big. Each thrust was tight and intense. Brody drove into her. She tried to match his strokes but in this position her movement was limited, which was probably what he wanted. He eased back and thrust deep in one hard, long stroke, which hit her G-spot. Denise moaned. Damn, she thought she was done after the last orgasm but apparently not.

Brody chuckled. "Greedy aren't you?"

"Mmm, little bit maybe, that's what happens when I have to go without you for two weeks," she said.

"Well I guess I'd better do a better job taking care of my woman."

Brody shifted his weight so each time he thrust he pounded against her G-spot. The cords in his neck stood out when he threw back his head and groaned out his release. He pulled back and drove forward one last time, dragging her along in his wake as a second orgasm ripped through her.

Panting to catch her breath, she dropped her legs down on either side of Brody. He rested his head against her chest. Denise sighed. She could quite happily stay this way forever.

Brody pushed up and kissed her lips. "Hold that thought," he said.

"How do you know what I'm thinking?" she asked.

"Because I'm thinking the same thing." He kissed her again. "Just let me get rid of this and I'll be right back," he said, indicating the condom.

"Hurry," she told him.

"You couldn't keep me away, honey."

Basking in the afterglow, Brody tucked one arm behind his head and stroked Denise's back with his other hand. No matter what else happened, this is where he belonged. With her.

Denise rested her arms on his chest and tucked her hands beneath her chin to prop herself up. Those amazing crystal-blue eyes of hers twinkled as she looked at him. "So I was thinking, since we're going to be equals in some of this stuff, what do you think of me cashing in on your name a little bit?"

"What'd you have in mind?" he asked.

"Umm...well...I was thinking maybe I could advertise that I trained your horse. Not just word-of-mouth advertising but real honest-to-god advertising."

His mind started racing as she spoke. That was it. The answer had been right there in front of him the entire time. He'd just been too wrapped up in his own crap to see it. He grabbed the back of her head and crushed her mouth to his. "That's perfect."

"What's perfect?"

"Using my name for this place."

Denise's forehead wrinkled. "What are you talking about?"

"How I can contribute. I get asked all the time to do roping seminars. What if I did them here instead of someplace else? We could really build it up into something fantastic."

"That would be amazing, Brody. If we had trained horses ready to go, endorsed by you, people would pay top dollar for them." Denise beamed at him. "That's perfect, build on both of our strengths to really maximize the business potential."

He grinned. "Partners."

"Equals," Denise replied.

He cupped the back of her head and pulled her down to meet his lips. Growing up, he'd never imagined his dreams would ever become a reality, but he'd finally found a place where he truly belonged. "Equals. I like that."

THE END

For upcoming releases, exclusive content, contests and giveaways, be sure to Subscribe to my newsletter Plus as a newsletter subscriber you'll get access to a newsletter subscriber-only FREE book.

Want a sneak peak at Kasey and Duncan's story, Round Up. Keep reading to read an excerpt.

EXCERPT FROM ROUND UP

What the hell was going on?

Kasey Davison watched the cab pull to a stop in front of the ranch house. A skinny woman with long, light brown hair slid out of the backseat. She stared up at the house while the driver pulled out her suitcase from the trunk and then drove away, leaving the woman standing alone.

Shit, so much for getting his work done. He pulled off his gloves and tossed them on the side of the wheelbarrow. As he approached the woman, he examined her from head to toe. She was attractive. A little on the skinny side for his liking, but overall, not bad. He took in the heeled boots, expensive looking jeans, and fancy purse and snorted. Definitely out of place on a dusty ranch.

"Can I help you?" he asked.

The woman looked up at the house again and chewed her full bottom lip. "Umm, I'm looking for Katherine McCray."

"She's not here."

"Do you know when she'll be back?"

"As a matter of fact, I do. She'll be back in about ten days."

Her shoulders sagged. "Ten days?" The woman looked defeated as she eyed the bag on the ground beside her. "Great," she muttered.

"There something I can help you with?"

"No, thanks." She grabbed the handle of her bag and turned towards the driveway. The wheels of the suitcase caught in on a rock and the bag tipped slightly before she could right it. Her head dropped forward, and she audibly sighed, then turned around. "Actually, can I borrow your phone to call the cab back? Mine died yesterday, and I haven't had a chance to charge it."

Kasey crossed his arms over his chest and stared at the woman. Who was this woman and what kind of person showed up unannounced and had the cab drop them off?

"Mind my asking why you're looking for Kat?"

"She still goes by Kat?" She smiled.

"Yep. So how do you know her?"

"We're friends."

Considering he'd never seen her before, they couldn't be that close of friends. She sure as hell hadn't been at the wedding. "Close are ya'?"

She chewed her bottom lip again and her eyes welled up. "We used to be. I haven't seen her in a while."

The way she stood there wringing her hands together all slouched into herself reminded him of a scared animal. His stomach knotted as he looked at her. *Shit, maybe he could ease up a bit.* "I'm Kasey and you are?"

"Oh, umm, I'm Julia." She glanced up at him beneath her lashes and flashed him a tight smile. He'd never seen lashes that long before. Kat always put a bunch of crap on her eyes to make her lashes look that long, but this woman didn't appear to have a lick of makeup on. His gut clenched as checked out the fresh-faced newcomer. Shit, if she put makeup on, she'd be a knockout.

"So, Julia, you and Kat used to be friends?"

"Yeah, we grew up together." She sighed. "We sort of lost touch over the years."

"And yet here you are, showing up on her doorstep with a suitcase?"

She snorted. "If you knew me, it wouldn't seem so strange."

He widened his stance and stared down at her. "Well, I don't know you, and it strikes me as more than a little odd."

Julia looked down at her shoes. "I'm sure it does. So, about that phone, can I borrow yours."

Just as he was reaching into his pocket, Duncan called out for him. "Kase?"

"Yeah, I'm out front," he yelled back.

Duncan rounded the corner. He sauntered towards them with that cocky swagger of his that Kasey liked so much. Even after all this time, he still enjoyed watching him walk. Duncan glanced towards the woman and grinned. "Well, hello there."

Julia blushed. "Hi," she murmured.

Duncan waggled his eyebrows and winked at him. The man never changed. Put an attractive woman in front of him and he couldn't seem to help himself from flirting.

"This is an 'old friend' of Kat's." Kasey air-quoted the 'old friend'. He still wasn't entirely sure what to think about this stranger showing up when Kat was away, claiming to be her friend.

"Oh yeah. So how come you weren't invited to the wedding?" Duncan asked.

"Kat got married?" she asked, her green eyes sparkled with joy.

"Sure did. She's away on her honeymoon right now?" Duncan told her.

"That explains why she's gone for ten days then." She gripped the handle of her suitcase again. "I guess I'll just get out of your way, then."

"Hang on." Duncan reached out and grabbed her arm. She flinched back.

He held out his hands, palms forward. "It's okay. I'm not going to hurt you."

"I didn't think you were," she said belligerently.

Kasey met Duncan's eyes. What was going on here?

"Look, if you're friends with Kat, we aren't just going to send you off without a place to go," Duncan said.

"We're not?" Kasey asked.

"No, we're not." Dunc glared at him.

"What are you going to do, then?" Julia asked.

Duncan shrugged. "We'll call her."

"You're going to call her on her honeymoon?" Julia's voice rose high in outrage.

"Sure, why not?"

"Because it's her honeymoon," she argued. Her eyes widened as if they were crazy for even suggesting something like that.

Duncan shrugged. "Clearly you don't know her husband. Justin is a control freak. He needs a daily check-in anyway, so he won't be too pissed if I call."

Julia warily eyed Duncan, then looked over at Kasey as if she wanted confirmation. He sighed. "It's fine."

Since Kasey still had his phone in his hand, he dialed. Justin answered and growled. "This better be good."

"Did I get you at a bad time?"

"It's my honeymoon. What do you think?"

"I think you're the one who wanted to check-in daily, dude."

"Yeah, but in case you forgot, I'm supposed to call you. So, what's up? Why the phone call?"

"Umm, is Kat available?"

"Kat?"

"Mmm hmm."

"Why do you want to talk to her?"

He sighed. "Just put her on."

"Fine," Justin grumbled.

While he waited for Kat to come to the phone, he looked at Julia, watching him avidly. She appeared relaxed, and not at all worried about how the conversation was going to go. She didn't look like she had anything to hide, but her whole behavior was a little on the weird side.

"Hello."

"Hi darlin', sorry to interrupt the honeymoon, but a friend of yours just showed up at the ranch."

"A friend of mine? Who?"

"She says her name is Julia."

"Julia? Julia Cragan?"

"I don't know," Kasey responded. He looked at the woman in question. "What's your last name?"

"Cragan."

"That's her," he told Kat.

"Oh my god, really?" Kat squealed. "How does she look?"

Typical woman. Not any kind of wondering why she showed up unannounced. No. How does she look? "I don't know. I've never seen her before," he grouched.

"Fine," she huffed. "Let me talk to her."

He looked at Julia and held out the phone. "She wants to talk to you."

She grabbed it from him and quietly began speaking. She walked a few feet away from them as she talked. Her voice pitched low so he couldn't make out what she was saying.

"So, what do you think?" Duncan asked.

"Weird."

Dunc smirked. "I meant, what do you think of her?"

Kasey eyed the other woman, the way her jeans clung to a surprisingly shapely ass. Her light brown hair hung past the middle of her back. She was definitely attractive, in a girl next door kind of way. But the way she had flinched when Duncan touched her was really what drew him in. There was a story there, he was sure. And he intended to find out what it was.

The woman in question walked back and handed the phone to Kasey. "Kat wants to talk to you," she said.

"Hey, Kat," he said.

"Julia is going to stay at the ranch until we get back from our honeymoon," Kat told him.

"Okay, is she sleeping in the main house, or do you want her to bunk with us?" he asked.

"Umm, probably the main house. She sounds off, like something is up with her and I would rather she didn't feel all invaded and scrutinized in case there's more to the story than she let on right now." Kat paused. "How does she look, not like is she pretty, that I already know, but like, how does she seem? You're good at reading people, so what's your take?"

Kasey looked over at the woman in question. Julia pulled her sleeves down over her hands and chewed her bottom lip as she watched him. She didn't have the outward confidence a beautiful woman in designer clothes would normally have. She reminded him of a wounded bird.

Conscious of his audience, Kasey replied. "Running, I think, but we'll get it sorted out. We'll take care of your friend for you until you get back. Tell Justin we have everything under control, and he can consider this his call for the day, so he's all yours."

Kat chuckled. "I'm sure he'll be happy to hear that."

If Kasey knew Justin, he could just imagine what he had on the agenda for today, so having uninterrupted time with Kat would definitely be appreciated. "Enjoy the rest of your day," he said as he hung up the phone.

He pocketed his phone and made eye contact with Duncan before turning to their guest. "So, it looks like you are bunking with us for the next 10 days."

Her eyes boggled, and she took a step away from him. "With you? What? No, I can't bunk with you," she stammered.

"Sorry, not with us, but here at the ranch with us. We'll put you in Kat and Justin's place until they get back. Then, if you are still here when they get home, we can figure something else out."

Duncan nodded his head. "Alright, follow me." He reached for her suitcase.

Buy Link

About Author

Lauren Fraser resides in British Columbia, Canada, with her husband, two children, and two dogs. When she's not busy writing, Lauren loves to spend time with her family outside—camping, hiking and paddle boarding.

Lauren writes about love and relationships in many different forms, but in the end, she's a sucker for a happy ending. She is multi-published and loves to hear from her readers. For the latest updates, visit her website.

Website http://www.laurenfraser.com
Newsletter: http://www.laurenfraser.com/newsletter

Also By

Letting Go

The Geek Next Door

Dani's Duo

Longing for Kayla

Too Hot

Sex, Sin and Surf

Aged to Perfection

Yielding for Him

www.ingramcontent.com/pod-product-compliance
Lightning Source LLC
Chambersburg PA
CBHW011041190726
48290CB00011B/2950

Explosive
Reactive Magic Book Four

Helen Vivienne Fletcher